C000257110

PICK THE WILDFLOWERS

Pick The Wildflowers

Tracy Lee Thompson

I. Dream Publishing

Also by Tracy Lee Thompson

Follow The Stars

Copyright © 2021 by Tracy Lee Thompson

All rights reserved. No part of this book may be reproduced in any manner whatsoever without written permission except in the case of brief quotations embodied in critical articles and reviews.

First Printing, 2022

To my husband, Stephen,
and my two boys, Bailey and Toby,
and to those who showed up in my dreams
and inspired them.

Prologue

I'm ninety-four. I don't feel ninety-four, but my crooked hands remind me of it every day. It's true what they say: time is the enemy. It strips away a day at a time, and soon age has slapped you down. Inside, I feel as if I haven't changed, but my reflection tells a different tale. The wrinkles came. My hair is thin and faded. Through the withered face staring back at me, I can see tiny snippets of the man I used to be.

My life has passed like a shadow. I've encountered my share of unexpected cruelties that life has to offer. What I've learned is that we get only two choices: Either we can let the circumstances drag us down and get left behind, or we can pick ourselves up and go on taking part in the most remarkable adventure called life.

When death shows his soulless face, I will not fear him. I know I've lived a long and full life. I have spun on this carousel of life and lovingly embraced those joyous occasions that caused my spirit to dance. On the flip side, my soul remembers the extreme pain I grappled with when it felt as if something inside of me had died. Sometimes I wish I could go back and erase all those awful moments, but that would create a different outcome. It took years for me to understand this, but by finally accepting the pain, I've healed.

This sterile white room has been my home for the past nine days. The day I arrived, the strong stench of disinfectant stung my nostrils and the heart monitor kept me awake at night. Now I don't seem to notice any of it.

My curiosity keeps me entertained. Visitors, patients, and even nurses congregate out in the hall, telling each other their secrets. I still hear everything, and my mind is still sharp. But that doesn't stop people treating me like a silly old coot.

With age comes invisibility. Society deems us unworthy participants. We're expected to sit on the side-lines and let the world pass by. They all seem to forget we've gained the wisdom and the skills that could help the next generation.

Often in the moments when I'm left alone in the semi-darkness of my room, I look back on my life. I can play it like an old film at will. In my mind, I watch myself grow younger. My hair returns to the sandy colour it once was. The wrinkles tighten and smooth as my face rejuvenates. My shoulders straighten. I am now, for the first time in many years, pain free. My memory wanders through the passage of time as if events from long ago happened only yesterday.

Retelling my story is an exercise for the soul. It brings me so much joy to share my fabulous milestones, to reveal those dark haunting hours, and to recall the days when my heart pulsed with a zest for excitement. But first, I should introduce myself. My name is Toby Mitchell, and my account of this journey starts with my first dance.

Seventeen

1

I'm standing with my older brother, Bill, along the main street. We are watching the townsfolk pile out of train carriages and parked cars. They look like tiny ants, dashing around, then falling into line to follow each other. It's my first town dance. There's a two-year difference between my brother and me. Some days he's my nemesis, the only villain in my world, but despite that, I admire the way he continually has my back. He's always loyal if a little overprotective. Even though he's three inches taller than I, people still mix the two of us up, often calling us by the wrong name. Perhaps it's our sandy-coloured hair and blue eyes that confuse them, but other than that, I don't see the similarities.

As Bill leads me at a steady pace down along the foot-path, my eyes fix on the grand hall in front. The towering building constructed of large stone blocks stretches out over a manicured lawn. Massive cathedral-like windows peek through long arms of green ivy. Undeniably, it's built to thrill the wealthy.

At the entrance, Bill and I weave our way through the crowd as we climb the wide stone steps. I follow Bill through the double wooden doors and into the auditorium. Amid the stream of people advancing in the same direction, I stop and suck in a sharp breath. Suspended in the middle of the hall is a magnificent chandelier, floating there like a flood-lit cloud. I blink in wonder as the crystal droplets splash tiny rainbow prisms across the walls and over the floor. Someone shoves me from behind, and I stagger forward. The crowd swells and presses in on me, and there's nothing I can do but flow with the current. I fret, wide-eyed with shock. From out of nowhere, an unseen hand comes in and drags me off to one side. I lift my head. It's Bill. I offer no resistance. We move our way through the crowd, treading on toes and bumping into shoulders. The stench of expensive perfume floating in the air is overpowering.

Bill yanks me free from the traffic flow, and we move off to one side.

"Jeez, Bill, is it always like this?" I fidget, readjusting my shirt.

"Yeah, but only at the start." As he speaks, his eyes roam around the room. "It's only because the rich are competing against each other for the best seats. It will calm down soon. You'll see."

"So what else should I prepare for?"

He folds his arms up over his chest and leans back against the wall. "Um ... let's start with the rules. Right. Rule number one." He lifts his forefinger. "You already know to keep clear of the rich. They stay on their side. We stay on ours."

"Why? What happens if you go over there?"

"Just listen." He looks up, his eyes blazing. "This is our side." He punctuates his words with hand gestures. "And that is theirs. You got it?"

"Yeah. You don't have to be an arse. I was only asking."

"Right. Rule number two." He holds up another finger. "If you meet a girl, don't dance with her all night."

"What!" My eyes narrow. "What does that mean?"

He draws a breath and sends another fiery glance. "Do you want to know the rules or not? Because I don't care if you have to find out the hard way."

"No. No—keep going. I didn't understand what you meant."

He sighs. "What I'm saying is, keep your options open. Don't dance with just one girl. Dance with many. I always do."

"Yeah, right," I say with a laugh. "And what's the third rule?" I cram my hands deep into my pockets and lean forward to make eye contact with him.

"What?"

"The third rule. You've told me only two."

His face hardens. "Because there are only two."

"So these are your made-up rules. I thought you were telling me the social guidelines."

"I don't know why I bother to tell you stuff." He glares at my face, one eyebrow cocked. "I wanted to help, but whatever. Go make an idiot of yourself. I don't care. I'm always up for a laugh."

I take a deep breath, turn my head, and notice the crowd has now thinned. Out the corner of my eye, I see Bill's friend, Sam, smiling as he walks towards us. The two of them became friends on their first day of school. I'm sure it was their excess energy and devilish behaviour that bonded them together. Some days, they tease and fiercely compete against each other, and then later they always come

7

together to discuss team tactics. I've lost count of how many times my mother has marched both of them back into town to apologise for their outrageous pranks. I guess you could say this freckle-faced boy is like another annoying brother to me.

Sam greets me with a nod and steps between my brother and me. "Hey, Toby, are you ready for it?" He turns his head away. "Bill, I hear the ladies are sick of seeing your ugly head around here."

"Nah, I find they can't get enough of this." Bill runs his fingers back through his hair.

"You're an idiot." Sam rolls his eyes. "But I guess I've always known that."

When the band begins to tune their instruments, I toss a side glance to the rows of girls sitting along the wall. The thought of approaching any of them scares the hell out of me. To be honest, I would prefer to deal with a black snake on a dirt track any day than find the courage to ask for a dance.

Whack!

Bill's hand thumps hard against my stomach, forcing the air out of my lungs. Leaning forward, I grasp my belly with both hands and suck in a breath. "What the hell, Bill!"

He stoops down so I can hear him over the band. "Well, you didn't answer me."

"I didn't catch what you said."

"I wanted to know if you've chosen a girl yet."

"No." I stand upright. Bill copies, and there's a smirk playing on his lips. "What do you want to know for?"

"So I don't ruin your chances by asking the same girl to dance."

"Yeah, whatever." I bite down on my bottom lip to avoid speaking to him. I have sported his game so many times. It's called "one-up," and all you have to do is embarrass the other guy and get one up on him. It's as easy as that.

"So which one is it?" Bill continues to play.

"I don't know."

"You sound a little nervous there, brother." He smirks. "Do you want me to line one up for you?"

"No!"

"Maybe I should show you how?" He leans in, relaxes his elbow on my shoulder, lifting his brows. "Well?"

I shove his arm away and straighten my shirt. The moment I look back, he's no longer standing next to me. I scan the room and spot him strutting over to some girls sitting along the wall. In all the exaggerated speeches he's told me over the years, he claims the ladies love him. But I'm familiar with the way the people of this town act towards us. Regardless of that, I still pay attention with keen interest to learn anything to help settle my nerves.

With each stride he takes, he looks even more awkward. Then he pauses in front of four girls and strikes an uncomfortable, stiff mannequin pose. In unity, all four heads lift, each giving an imperious glare followed by a look of disgust.

"What the hell is he doing?" Sam shakes his head and smiles.

A chuckle erupts from me as I look back in time to witness four feminine faces souring. But Bill's determination only spurs him on. He stays planted on the spot and starts up a one-sided conversation.

It's fascinating, standing there watching him make a fool of himself. It's only a matter of seconds before the blond-haired girl stands. Her voice can be heard all over the room. "We said no! Now move away. Do you want me to get my father?"

Rows of heads strain to stare over at him. I watch as his eyes flicker amongst the faces. With nothing else left to do, he turns and walks towards us. He seems mortified. His face and his ears are as red as the rose boutonnieres pinned to the suits of the wealthy. I can't believe it. My brother, the one

9

who would embarrass Sam or me at any chance he could, has finally found his karma. I watch him walk. Not once does he look over at us.

Sam and I share another quick glance. The laughter explodes from our mouths and echoes out across the hall. Large tears flow and drip down over our cheeks.

Seconds later, when Bill steps in alongside us, I have to squeeze my lips together to imprison the chuckle I feel in the back of my throat. "Wow," I taunt. "You are amazing. How do you do it?"

A cackle spills from Sam.

At that precise moment, the orchestra starts up, and couples by the dozens stroll out onto the dance floor.

"So ... Um ..." I add, leaning into him, yelling out over the music. "Do you have to go back over there to get her or is she meeting you out there?" A smile creeps onto my face. "Well?"

"Whatever." Bill grits his teeth. "Say whatever you want, brother, you can't even approach a girl! So how stupid are you?"

"Oh, come on, Bill. Don't be so serious." Sam nudges his arm with his elbow. "Toby was only joking."

"Well, if he thinks he can do it better, then don't let me stop him." Bill turns his head and stares straight at me. "Come on, big shot, show me."

"Okay, I will." In a flash, the realisation sinks in that, once again, I have accepted his challenge. Why do I fall for it every time? Why do I have to prove him wrong all the time? When will I learn? I dart my eyes around the room and take in the sea of dancers. They glide weightlessly as if the music somehow now controls their souls.

Suddenly, my breath catches in my throat. Out of an entire roomful of dancers, my eyes gravitate to a girl in a blue dress.

She has stolen the air right out of my lungs. In my trance-like state, I watch her waltz around the room. She never misses a step. Her movements flow freely as she whirls in and out and then slips in under her partner's arm. Like her, he is about money. His lavish suit and polished shoes prove it. Under the bright light, I gaze freely at her, noting the way her long, brown, wavy hair shifts across her shoulders. I'm fascinated, and for the first time in my life, something twitches inside me.

It's not long until Bill taps me on the shoulder, making me jump. I turn my head and catch both their brazen smiles that expose just about every tooth in their mouths.

"So ... I see you found a girl." Bill rubs his palms together. "And she's on the wrong side of the hall. Oh, this should be interesting."

Sam turns his head, meeting my gaze. "I wouldn't bother with that one, Toby."

"Why? Do you know her? What's she like?"

"How would I know?" Sam's eyes narrow. "I'm just stating those snooty brats don't even know we exist."

"But," Bill intervenes, holding up his forefinger, "if you believe you have a chance with daddy's little rich girl, then off you go. You said you'd show me." His smile widens, and the dimples appear on his cheeks. "Well, off you go."

"Come on, Toby. You can do it." Sam jerks his thumb at me and then laughs.

As I slide my hands into my pockets, I realise they're hatching a plan. My brain scrambles for a way to get out of this predicament. Within minutes, the music fades. I turn my head and watch her leave the dance floor. She disappears into the crowd that is gathering on the other side. It's then that Bill says out loud.

"Now's your chance, brother."

With nothing left to do, I take in a big gulp of air, turn sideways, and search for her among the groups gathered on the other side of the hall.

The room buzzes around me as people chat loudly and men flock to collect refreshments from tables and quickly carry them back to their dance partners. I step forward, knowing everything hinges on what I do and how I do it. If I fail, I will never hear the end of it. I strain my neck until I eventually locate her hitching up her long white gloves as she talks to three other girls. My heart pounds in my chest in an abnormal rhythm as I start to move forward.

My stomach shifts when I realise I'm about to tread over that invisible line that divides the social status in two.

I stop and quickly glance back over my shoulder. Bill and Sam stand perfectly still, eyeing me with anticipation. A second later, Bill lifts his arm and flicks his wrist, a signal for me to hurry along.

Deflated, I swivel my head back and let my eyes focus on her for a second. I take a moment to realise that the noise nearby is actually me gasping for air. As I continue across the floor, every head turns to gawk at me. Now silence follows me as conversations dissolve. Everything seems to be happening in slow motion. I am mindful of the anonymous stunned faces glaring at me, aware of the quietness swelling in the hall, conscious that my heart is bouncing off my chest plate. A woman standing over in the corner whispers something to the person next to her. I wonder what she said.

On autopilot, I take a swift glance at the girl who is now only a few feet away. I freeze with shock when I discover her eyes are homed in on me. In my nervous state, I whip my hands out of my pockets. Now I'm unsure where to put them. A bead of sweat rolls down the side of my face, and I quickly swipe it away with my fingers. Up close, she is beautiful—her porcelain skin, her deep-green eyes, a light scattering of freckles over the bridge of her nose that extend out over her cheeks.

I seize a few seconds to try to think of what I should say to her, but the words seem to warp and elongate in my brain. I blink and swallow loudly. My mouth opens briefly before I close it. Again I try to speak, but no words come. I peer past the girl to the multitude of people behind her and catch their eyes wandering up and down over my body. It is daunting standing there amidst the wealthy in their overpriced garments and sparkling jewels when I'm dressed in my best attire, the clothes my mother made. At one point, someone laughs.

Once I hear the band start again, I allow myself to soak into the moving dancers. I need to hide my embarrassment, my absolute humiliation. What was I thinking? I need the ground to swallow me whole.

When I manage to get my legs working again, I pivot my body around and scuttle forward. Through the shifting dancers, I catch tiny flashes of Bill and Sam, who are doubled over in harsh fits of laughter. Silently, I curse myself for being their light entertainment. One ragged breath after another pumps through my lungs. As my eyes flicker between the two of them, I conjure up the many ways in which I can get them back. Nothing comes to mind; my brain must still be numb from what just happened.

I've almost reached them when Bill straightens up his shoulders and quickly taps Sam on the arm. "Shhh!" He clears his throat and smacks his lips together. His twisted cocky smile annoys the hell out of me. In fact, his whole face annoys me. It's always full of such arrogance when he plays his stupid games.

"So, brother." He bites down on his bottom lip as if keeping his raucous laughter contained. "When's the dance?" A laugh rumbles its way out of his throat.

Sam chuckles and slaps the side of his leg.

"Yeah, yeah, all right. You can make fun of me, but at least I tried."

Sam tilts his head. "You failed don't you mean?"

"Say what you want, but you two idiots can't get a girl from our side, so what does that say about you."

Their boasting laughter dies faster than a flame doused with water. Bill sniffs and swipes a finger in under his eyes. Sam blinks as he takes a breath. I wait for either one of them to add something—anything—but they don't. Next, a heavy silence settles over us. Now it's uncomfortable. They glare at me through narrow eyes. The tightness of their jaws implies they are not the gracious losers they pretend to be. Slowly, I slink away from them.

From where I now stand, near the front entrance, I can see everything, including the girl in the blue dress. As she waltzes with that boy, she holds the hem of her gown daintily between her fingers and thumb. She skims a look in my direction. The butterflies roam in my stomach. I swallow nervously. In a quick sequence of movements, she rotates back into him, and together they sashay across the floor. Moments later, the melody of the music spins them away.

Behind me, a commotion erupts. I twist round to find two men squaring off, spilling their alcohol all over the floor. At least ten men rush in, grabbing the two offenders by the arms and hauling them back into different directions. By the time I swing my head around, the music has stopped.

Alone, and standing directly opposite me on the other side of the hall, I notice her watching me. I commit to her gaze. In an instant, she bites down on her bottom lip, and just before she turns away, she smiles. Then, from out the corner of my eye, I catch suit boy walking towards her, a glass of punch in hand. I peer back over, trying to make eye contact with her again, but she's glancing around the room. The boy stops in front and offers her the punch. No words seem to pass between them. They remain there sipping their drinks in silence.

I casually turn my head to find Bill and Sam standing there, watching me, grinning, but I don't care. For the rest of the night, I stay there, sharing tiny glances with her. After that night, my life would never be the same.

2

A ray of sunlight spears through my bedroom window, warming my skin. Usually at this point, I'm up, dressed, and cooking breakfast out in the kitchen. Today, however, I don't want to think about the tasks ahead while I still have the image of the girl in my head. I need to know her name and find out why she kept looking at me. My heart flutters in my chest just thinking about her.

Through the silence of the house, a fist pounds hard, like gunfire, on my bedroom door.

I jolt up onto my elbow.

"Are you getting up or what?"

I relax when I establish it's only Bill. My first thought is to shout out and tell him to get lost. The next is one of irritation for disturbing such pleasing thoughts.

Thump! Thump!

"Did ya hear what I said? It's well after six."

"Yeah, yeah! I heard ya." I sit up and hang my legs over the side of the bed.

"Well come on, we don't have all day."

As I take a deep breath, I come to realise my thoughts are ridiculous. For she will only ever be my crush. Society dictates that the noticeable differences between us and the standards of the local community will guarantee she will never be mine.

I don't move off the bed until I hear the old floorboards groan down the hall.

Dressed, I shift out into the corridor that leads into the kitchen.

First, let me tell you about my father. He left us when I was eight years old, leaving my mother as the sole carer. One day he came home from work, walked into the house as he'd done a hundred times before, but this time it was different. This time when Bill and I raced over to give him the customary hug, he shoved us both aside. He then proceeded to pack up what few belongings he could carry. Then he left. I remember sitting out on the front porch steps, watching him walk down the curve of the drive until he melted into the land. Every day after that, I'd come home from school and sit out there on that same step, waiting, hoping for him to return. He never did.

With our father gone, Bill had to finish up his schooling and find a job. He was eleven at the time. Our neighbour, John Picker, helped by employing him to work on his farm. It was a tough slog for a young kid, but with Picker's help and guidance, the job soon came easy.

Two years on, my mother's mind began to slip. One day, when she became disorientated and couldn't remember which house to clean, the whole town buzzed with rumours that something dark and twisty had possessed my mother's mind. From that day on, she became an outcast and therefore unemployable. Today it's known as the early onset of dementia.

With my mother's wage gone, it was now my turn to leave school and find a job. Once again, Picker was there to help.

As soon as I enter the kitchen, I find Bill tossing a handful of twigs into the roaring flames in the stove. Over at the end of the table, my mother sits sewing one of her patchwork quilts. I move further into the room. Bill pops his head up quickly.

"Where have you been? I'm starving. I thought I might have to cook breakfast myself."

"Yeah," I say with a laugh, lifting my eyebrows. "Don't forget the last time when you burned everything and smoked up the house."

"I don't remember it being that bad."

"Ah, yes, it was."

As I approach my mother, she continues to push the needle in and out of the fabric. Little by little, her mind has slowly smudged out the vital elements in her life. I am grateful it hasn't robbed her of this one thing she finds so comforting.

Stopping in front of her, I crouch down and stare up into her thin face. It takes her a moment to set the patchwork quilt down in her lap before she elevates her head. Her blue eyes fix on mine. Some days this is our only form of communication. But not today. Today the edges of her mouth are curling into the most glorious smile. It's one of her good days. I am grateful she remembers me.

"Toby, my sweet boy." She lifts her hands and cups the sides of my face. "You're growing up so fast. You're almost as tall as Bill."

"Yeah almost." I stand and plant a kiss on the top of her head. "Won't be too long before he's looking up at me."

Bill closes the hatch of the fire and stands up. "You're such a funny brother. As if that's ever gonna happen." He keeps his eyes on me as I move around the room.

From off the top shelf, I grab the frying pan and gather up enough supplies to make breakfast.

"Hey, what happened to you last night?" Bill yells out.

I glance over my shoulder. "Why? What do you mean?"

"Well, we couldn't find you when it was time to leave." He pulls a chair out from under the table and sits. "Did you leave early because we embarrassed you?"

I ignore him and turn back to the stove. While I work, I sense his eyes still watching me.

"You know we were only having a bit of fun last night." He lets out a laugh. "If you could have seen your face with that girl, you would have laughed too. That's all I'm saying."

I stride over to the table and start cutting yesterday's bread into thick slices.

Bill continues. "I can't believe you thought you had a chance with that girl." He reaches across and steals a slice of bread from off the plate.

"I didn't."

"So why did you do it then?" He rips off a small piece and stuffs it into his mouth.

"I don't know. Probably to prove you wrong."

"Well, you didn't." He looks down at his hands and peels off another piece. "Those girls care only about money. Trust me on that." He lifts his head, sighs, and looks straight into my eyes. "You have to realise it's not just about the money thing now. It's also about those rumours. No one wants anything to do with us."

I stop cutting and stare down at him. "Then why did you ask those girls to dance?"

"To be honest, it was only to get you going." He smiles to himself. "And I did. But sometimes I do it to annoy them. They're never gonna change their opinions of us, so why not make it fun?"

"I don't understand why you think it's a game." I place the knife down on the table and return to the cooker.

"Oh, you need to lighten up. I only do it to make them feel uncomfortable. Didn't you see the way they were all watching us last night?"

His words punch me in the gut. Was that the reason she observed me? To make sure I stayed away from her?

"Look, all I'm saying is give it a go and you'll see how entertaining it is." He stands, and the chair scrapes back across the floor. A second later, he appears at my side. "How long until that's ready?"

"Soon." I let out a sigh. "Bill, I need you to come into town to help carry back supplies."

He turns away uninterested. "Ah, shit, I didn't want to go in there today."

"Well, we have to, so just do it."

With breakfast out of the way, we make the two-mile hike into town. Even though it's mid-morning, the sun licks at our faces and soaks through our clothes. Beads of sweat trickle down our spines, drenching the lower parts of our shirts. The air is dry and sickly, not the typical weather we usually have in spring.

Twenty minutes later, when we reach the outskirts of town, I look up and take in the sea of people filling up the footpaths along the sides of the wide main street. Most are trying to escape the heat by standing under rickety wooden shopfront awnings or under the boughs of trees.

As we make our way through the crowd, I lift my head and take in the many assorted faces staring at us. Once again, their expressions of disgust show we are not welcome here. Some people sneer while others turn their heads away in disgust.

I turn my head to glance at Bill, who walks closely beside me. He offers a brief smile and then suddenly winks. "Take your time, folks. We're here all day. No need to soak it all in now." A smirk settles across his lips. It's a chance for him to have some fun.

Further on, we pass the post office and the city bank. Just as we're about to cross the road, Bill's hand slaps my back.

"Dammit, Bill." I spin around. "Stop doing that!"

"Look!" He points across the street. "There's your spoilt baby blue from last night."

Just the mere mention of her makes my heart thump in my chest. "Yeah, right. I'm not falling for that one." I force my hands into my pockets and twist back around, knowing he's trying to get one up on me. "Let's get the food and just go home. It's too hot."

"No, brother." He races up in front and tugs on my arm. "Look! I'm not lying."

Even as I stare at him, there's doubt in my mind. I let out a sigh, bracing myself for his practical joke. "Bill, if you're trying to get one—" Time abruptly collapses. Nothing else seems to exist as I gaze intently at this girl, noting the way she lifts her hand up to tuck a stray piece of hair in behind her ear.

Bill's voice carries me back to the moment. "Well, are you going to make a fool of yourself again?" He lets out a chuckle.

"Quick, Bill." I turn around and hold my palm out to him. "Give me a penny."

He lowers his eyes down to my hand. "What are you doing?"

I don't answer.

He stands there, eyes shifting from the girl to me. "You're not gonna give her a penny, are you?"

"Just give it to me." I wave my palm out in front.

Laughing, he shakes his head. "Um ... I'm pretty sure she doesn't need a penny. She's loaded!"

"I'm not giving her a bloody penny. Now just give me one."

"Okay, okay." He fishes around in his pocket. "You know she'll only laugh at you. Trust me on this."

The moment he pulls his hand out of his pocket, I snatch the penny from his fingers. I'm off. My feet hammer on the earth as I plough down the street. Angry pedestrians curse at me as I push my way through the crowd that's moving in both directions. But I don't care. My one aim is to get to the grocer's store.

Within minutes, I'm back, standing in front of Bill with a cold bottle of sarsaparilla in my hand.

"What the hell are you doing? Tell me you're not going over there. Have you forgotten what happened last night when you were humiliated?"

"No, I haven't forgotten because you won't let me." I swallow loudly. "But, Bill, I have to do this."

"What is it with this girl?" He clicks his tongue and shakes his head. "You'll only make an idiot of yourself again." He laughs out loud. "Oh, I can't wait to see this."

"No. You have to go."

"No, I don't."

"Yes, you do."

He folds his arms up over his chest. "But you said I have to help with the food, remember?"

"Stop it. Don't pretend now that you care about that. You didn't even want to come into town with me." I turn my head and take in the group of individuals eyeing me because I raised my voice. Embarrassed, I lower my head and swirl the gravel under my feet to allow enough time to compose myself.

In the stillness, I hear the hum of car engines.

By the time I lift my gaze, the crowd has already shifted. I reach into my pocket to retrieve the shopping list. "Just get whatever you can carry."

He says nothing as he snatches the list from my hand.

"Bill, I know you think it's stupid, but I have to do this."

His face softens. "You know that girl will only humiliate you. Trust me. I've been there before."

"Yes, she probably will, but if I don't try, then I will always wonder." I glance over at the girl and then back at him before sighing. "But I can't do this if I know you're waiting here watching me."

Bill bites down on his bottom lip. His eyes hold a muted understanding. "Okay, I'll go. But don't say I didn't warn you."

He turns and walks away. My eyes stay glued on his departing back until he vanishes around the corner. As I ponder the assignment ahead, a lump of nothing forms in the back of my throat. Slowly, I pivot. Despite the queasiness I feel in my stomach, I shuffle forward.

I pass families with dawdling toddlers, people stopping to take part in all kinds of conversations before shifting back into the rat race. Children chase each other through the street. Another quick glance at the girl, another explosion of heart palpitation. My hand trembles now in a way I can't control. The sticky liquid spills from the bottle, dribbling down over my hand and through my fingers. By the time I steady my shaking hand, the children have raced around me twice and are now progressing back down the street. Nearby a car horn toots. I spook, more liquid leaks from the bottle.

A few more steps, another glance. She's talking to the same girls she was with last night.

I'm less than three feet away. I move up onto the shopfront decking. The aging boards creak under my feet. Four sets of eyes swing my way. Immediately, my heart thumps so hard it feels as if it's beating outside my body. I can't think. The anxiety overload is too much to take. *Oh, god, think of something ... anything. They're watching you.* I shove my arm out in front. "Would you like some?"

All eyes, in unison, peer down to the drink in my hand. Without saying a word, their eyes pop back up to my face. I swallow and drop my head. Glancing down at the bottle with horror, I find it's almost empty.

"No ... No." It's not what you think." I glance upwards. "I swear to you I have had none. I spilled it on the way over. Oh, I'm sorry I shouldn't say *swear* in front of you. I'm sorry. Please, you gotta understand that I haven't touched it." Finally, I gain control over my waffling mouth by pressing my lips together.

Through the awkward silence, I sense their unspoken disapproval. Why have I done this? I am so stupid to think someone like her would want anything to do with me. I shift on my feet and lower my eyes. Only then I notice my hand's still extended out in front of her. At a quick pace, I yank the bottle into my chest. Why didn't I listen to Bill? He's probably standing somewhere on the corner watching this scenario unfold, laughing at me. Twice now I have embarrassed myself in front of this girl. What must she think? Should I walk away or wait here until they leave? Then, to my surprise, I hear the softest voice.

"Is that sarsaparilla?"

My eyes uplift to find her smiling at me. "Yes. Yes, it is."

"Is it cold?"

"Yes." I nod too quickly. "I just got it over at Tilly's store. Would you like some?"

"Oh, yes, please." She glances around the group before stretching out her hand. "A drink can be most refreshing on a day like today, don't you think?" She accepts the bottle and rests the top against her cherry lips.

As her head tips back, my eyes skim over her beautiful face, along her thin jawline, down over her delicate neck. My fascination causes me to stare. Within seconds after she lowers her head, I turn my face away. Smack bang, three sets of eyes scowl with horror. The bitterness almost hurls me back. Each mouth hardens into a thin line as their eyes, filled with disgust, roam down over my body. My insides tighten as I swallow, but I stay there, defiantly waiting them out.

The tall girl in the middle uses her hand to smooth the ruffles on the front of her dress. "Let's go, girls. We don't want people to think we're mixing with the likes of him." She delivers one last inspection before making a tutting sound and then storms off across the street. It's not long before the other two girls depart and quickly race after her.

I strain my neck watching the trio make their way through the procession of cars rolling down the avenue. As I wait, I speculate that the girl in front of me will soon accompany them.

The seconds tick by. Into the silence, a car door slams, and still she lingers. When she raises the bottle up to take another sip, I turn my face to view her. Sarsaparilla escapes out the side of her mouth and dribbles down over her chin. She giggles. I smile. The moment eases.

"Oh, I'm such a klutz." She wipes the fluid from her chin. "I'm sorry about those girls. I don't understand why my sister carries on like that." She grins and stares at me for the longest time. "Oh dear, where are my manners." She extends her free hand. "I'm Hildy. Hildy Baxter."

"Hello, Hildy." I shake her hand. The butterflies wander around in my stomach. "My name is Toby."

"Yes, I already know who you are."

"You do?" My eyes narrow as I let go of her hand. "I assume you've heard the gossip?" I pass this question off, already comprehending the outcome of what is about to happen.

"Yes, I have." She lifts a brow. "But I don't listen to silly gossip. I like to find out the truth for myself." She taps her nails against the bottle. "So, Toby, when I work it all out, you'll be the first to know."

"Okay." I smile. "I can live with that."

"All right then." She pushes her hair back behind her shoulders. "Tell me, what do you usually do on a hot day like this?"

"Well." I draw my brows together. "Normally, I cool off at the river."

"So, why aren't you there now?"

"I had to come in and grab a few things at the store first, and then I saw you standing here, and I thought ..." I immediately stop myself when I realise I'm babbling. "Anyway, I wanted to come and say hello."

"Hello." She nods. "Tell me, what's it like?"

"You mean the river?"

"Yes. I've never been. I'm not allowed to go anywhere

near it. It's not right for a lady to dip her toes in public … apparently." She rolls her eyes. "That's what my parents tell me."

"I go there every day, regardless of the weather. It's one of my favourite places."

"Every day?" She shakes her head. "What could you possibly do there every day?"

"Sometimes I go there just to relax—you know, to figure out stuff. Other times I go for a swim. You should come and see it sometime."

She catches her bottom lip in between her teeth. "Are you going soon?"

"Yeah. But I don't go down to Cooper's Bridge. Part of the river flows near my house. I go there."

"Oh." She concentrates for a moment. Her eyes never leave my face. "Can I come with you?"

"If you want to you can."

Her face lights up with a smile. "Yes, I would like that very much."

I half turn and gesture with my hand. "Well, it's this way."

She nods, smiles, and then steps forward. "Did you want a drink?"

"No, you can have it. I bought it for you."

Together, we take our time moving down the road. Those who are near us stop and stare. As we walk, I worry about our conversation, that somehow I will have nothing to say and she will find me boring. But my doubts don't last too long because, in the end, I can't get a word in. Hildy tells me all about her family and how they moved here a little over a year ago. She's just turned sixteen, and even though she didn't want a coming-of-age party, her parents still threw one because it is what the society circle wanted.

The walk home that day is everything. I can't stop myself from stealing glances at her profile. She is captivating—the way her face lights up when she speaks, the way she turns her head and smiles at me. I adore her. And in that precise moment, I know I love her—right then and there.

3

It takes a good thirty minutes for us to arrive outside our family property. I step forward, reach my hand up over the metal gate, and jiggle the lock. The gate swings open. I stand aside to allow Hildy to enter. After I clamp the barrier back into place, I lead her down the curve of the drive.

As we walk, I fear she will take one look at my family home, notice the deprived life I have compared to hers, and decide I am not worthy of her company. Hildy's voice comes to me through the maze of my thoughts.

"Toby, can I ask why you pin the gate when there's nobody out here?"

"It's because of my mother." I glance at her. "I'm not exactly sure what you've heard because there are so many rumours. But, one day when Bill and I finished our work shifts, we came home, and she wasn't here. We searched everywhere—

the river, the tall grass, the wildflowers—and still we couldn't pinpoint her location." I inhale and slowly release the air from my lungs as I grasp the abnormality of discussing my mother with a girl I'd only just met. "It wasn't until Picker—he's our neighbour," I say pointing east, "came down the driveway with her in his truck."

"Why? Where had she been?"

"He had found her in town. She wandered in to collect the mail and then forgot where she was. Picker saw her standing in the middle of the street, all confused and upset. The entire township had gathered. For some reason, they all felt it was okay to treat her like she was some circus freak."

"And no one thought to help her?"

"No. Why would they after everything they've done?" I veer my gaze away from her and kick a loose stone down along the path. "I'm not sure what we would have done if Picker hadn't found her."

"I'm so sorry, Toby."

"So, after that, Bill fixed the latch, and now my mother can't open it." I turn my head and capture her gaze.

"I understand." She smiles.

I smile back and quickly change the subject. "Well, this is where I live."

Her eyes skim away from me and over to the weathered white home. From where we stand, and with the help of the perfectly placed sun, we can't see the peeling paint falling off the walls or the rotten floorboards scattered across the front porch. Even the old majestic gum next to the house, with its low hanging branches, and the added pop of colour from the overgrown roses make the place look somehow welcoming.

While she surveys the scenery, I study her. Her face stays motionless as the silence lingers. Now I am getting nervous.

"It's beautiful," Hildy says, turning her head.

"I know it's not much, but it's the only place I've ever known."

"No. No, it's perfect. Really it is, Toby." Her lips move into the most glorious smile, and I see the truth in her eyes. "So you've lived here all your life?"

"Yep. Every day. I was born here."

"Oh, you must have such wonderful memories of this place. I've nothing like that." She glances across to the house. "My parents are always moving around, so I've never lived in any of our homes for more than two years. You're lucky. I can't recall any fond memories from any of those places."

I find her comment exceedingly odd as I wonder about her life. Why wouldn't she have special memories? Her privileged life should hold so many.

"Toby, may I ask you something?"

"Sure." I come back to the moment.

"Is it possible for me to meet your mother?"

Panic jolts through me like a lightning bolt. No one ever wants anything to do with my mother. I stare blankly at her for a few more seconds, blinking.

"If you would prefer that I didn't, then I understand."

"No, no, it's ..." I glance over to the house. "Some people get a little uncomfortable around her." Now I'm conscious that my tone may have been a little harsh. My eyes slowly find their way back to her.

"Of course. I understand."

Biting down on my bottom lip, I think how rare it is for someone to show interest in my mother. How strange it is to see eyes that hold no judgement. "You can meet her."

"Are you sure?"

"Yeah." I nod. "I'm sure."

"Oh, thank you, Toby. I would like that."

We make our way across the yard and up four weatherworn steps. The sweet scent of potted pansies swirls through the air. As we walk the length of the porch, we pass two wooden chairs that are so scarred from the weather they've turned grey. Stopping over at the front door, I look back over my shoulder. Hildy looks up and smiles. With a fumbling hand, I reach up and pull open the screen. It greets me with a familiar squeak. I step off to one side so Hildy can enter the house.

Inside, the living room is cluttered with an outdated lounge and matching chair. Over on the back wall, a large mahogany cupboard stands, stuffed with books, small trinkets, and a few framed photographs. For the moment, Hildy seems content observing the room. I keep my eyes on her as she walks behind the old lounge, tracing her fingertips across the patchwork quilt draped over the back of the seat. She lifts her head. Her eyes fixate on the cabinet at the end of the room.

"May I have a look at your photos?"

"Yes, please do." I move into the middle of the room.

Sliding my hands down into my pockets, I stare openly at her as she picks up a metal frame. She studies the photograph for a moment and then sets it down to move onto the next one. Then, from down the hall, we hear the faint sound of voices. She places the frame down and turns towards me.

"Is that your family?"

"Yes. Bill's out in the kitchen with my mother. Did you still want to be introduced?"

"Bill's your brother, right?"

"Yep, he's my annoying brother."

A smile stretches over her face. "If it's okay with you, I would like to meet him too."

"Sure, that's fine," I nod. It takes me a few good seconds to realise I'm staring. With that, I spin around and lead her down the shadowed hall towards the kitchen. As I walk, I can't help but wonder what Bill will think when he sets eyes on her. I silently laugh, hoping to get one up on him.

When I'm almost there, I sneak a peek back over my shoulder. Hildy has paused halfway down the hall, looking at the photographs hanging on the walls. I stop and wait for her in the open doorway. As Bill crosses the kitchen, he catches sight of me standing there. He stops and grins.

"Well, well, you're finally home." He collects the kettle from the stove and then makes his way over to the table. "So, brother, did you end up using your charm? Did you get the kiss of your dreams?" He gives a comical laugh.

I open my mouth to inform him about Hildy, but before I can get a word out, he holds his palm up and cuts me off.

"No, let me guess." He looks down and pours the hot water into the teapot. "Daddy's little girl wanted nothing to do with you. Am I right? I'm right, aren't I?" He lifts his face. "You need to listen. You're never gonna get someone like that, brother. They only care about how much money people have." He scoots back over to the cooker and sets the kettle down. "Do you know what I think?"

"No, Bill, why don't you tell me what you think?"

"I say forget that spoilt brat. She isn't worth it. None of them are."

I fold my arms over my chest and lean my shoulder against the door. There is no possible way I can hold off the smirk any longer. Slowly, it stretches over my mouth.

A second later, Bill stops, his brows creased. "What?"

"Oh, it's nothing."

"Then why does ya face look like—" Bill's face drops the moment Hildy steps in next to me. His eyes quickly shift between Hildy and me.

"Hildy," I add with great delight. "I want you to meet my brother, Bill."

Hildy extends her arm and walks into the kitchen. "Hello, Bill. It's a real pleasure to meet you."

Bill stands there, open-mouthed. His eyes follow her as she crosses the room. After she stops in front of him, he accepts her hand and leaks a silly giggle. I've never encountered this sort of behaviour from him before. I only wish Sam could be here to witness it.

Hildy continues to talk. "We were on our way to the river. I wanted to pop in and say hello to your mother. But I am glad you are here, Bill."

For the moment, Bill is silent. Hildy waits there, occasionally glancing down to their joined hands. The seconds tick by. Hildy tosses a look back in my direction. Bill's eyes slowly follow. It is only now that Bill realises he's still shaking Hildy's hand. In a flash, he whips his hand away and makes a mad dash for the door.

Just as Bill walks by, he lifts his face. I sense the discomfort, but I don't care. I give a tooth-baring grin.

"Shut up, brother," he mumbles out the side of his mouth and rushes out the door.

Hildy turns, her face holds confusion. "Did I do something to upset him?"

"No." I laugh, knowing for sure he was upset with himself because I got one up on him. "Oh, I wouldn't worry about that. He'll get over it." But I know differently. My brother never lets anything go. His need for revenge will gnaw on his soul until payback is served. I smile and move across the room.

When I reach my mother's side, I lean in and lightly tap her arm. She positions the quilt down onto her lap and lifts her chin.

"Mum, there's someone here who'd like to meet you."

Her eyes dart away from me and land on Hildy.

"Mum, this is Hildy." I turn my head. "Hildy, this is my mum, Hazel."

Hildy moves forward and kneels down, eyes level with my mother's. "Hello, Hazel. It's a real thrill to meet you."

My mother draws in a breath, and for a little while, she appears lost, deep in thought as her eyes roam over Hildy's face. "Have we met before?"

"No, this is the first time." Her tone is soft and friendly. "Let me start by saying I think your quilts are exquisite."

My mother drops her gaze down to her lap and considers Hildy's statement for what seems like a long time. "Do you sew quilts too?"

"Oh, no. I wouldn't know where to start." Hildy laughs.

"It looks hard, but it's not. I can teach you if you like?"

"Oh ... I would like that very much." Hildy stands and helps herself to a chair at the end of the table. Just when she's about to sit, I reach out and settle my hand down on her shoulder.

"You don't have to do this, you know?" I whisper out the side of my mouth.

"I know," Hildy says. "But I want too."

4

For more than an hour, Hildy stays with my mother. As I watch her, I can't see those self-absorbed traits that Bill has often talked about in girls like her. She accepts my mother for who she is. No one else has bothered to do that, especially in this community, for a good many years. From that point on, I don't feel the need to prove myself worthy anymore.

I feel the freedom of just being myself as I lead her down the front porch steps. We make our way across the yard, walk past the old shed, and arrive at the worn-out path that snakes its way through the tall grass. Just before we enter the grass, I turn back around to Hildy.

"Now, when we go in here, we need to stay as quiet as we can."

"Why? What's in there?"

"You'll see soon enough. Don't worry, it's all good. Trust me. You're going to love it." I offer a reassuring smile and go onwards, stepping onto the narrow trail.

As we advance, the tall blades of grass scrape against the sides of our legs, creating rustling sounds that break through the stillness. Seconds later, a flock of parrots bursts out of the grass, and the colourful birds take flight up into the bluest of skies.

I spin around. "Come on let's go!"

She accepts my proffered hand, and we're off, sprinting and weaving our way down the track. The silence is shattered. Birds by the hundreds explode out of the foliage. We halt. She releases my hand and tilts her head back. Cupping her palms up over her brows, she inspects the birds soaring overhead. I watch her face light up as they glide gracefully through the air. They loop to the right, then dart to the left, showing off their painted feathers. And as quickly as they arrived, they bolt back across the sky to merge as one with the horizon.

"Wow! That was incredible!" Hildy says, steadying her breathing.

"Well, if you liked that, you're gonna love the next thing."

"Why? What is it?"

"No, you must wait." I raise my eyebrows and grin. "It's a surprise."

"Tell me, Toby."

"No. Not yet. Close your eyes."

"What?"

"Just close your eyes."

There's a moment of silence in which I notice Hildy's face flush a shade of pink right before she closes her eyes. I position myself in next to her, cradling her elbow with my hand.

"Don't open them until I tell you."

"I won't. Are we almost there?"

"Yeah," I add, steering her through the last patch of greenery.

When we progress into the nearby meadow, I let go of her arm and slide my hands down onto her tiny waist, guiding her into place.

"Can I open them now?"

"No. Not yet. In a minute." I move into position so I can see her face. "Okay. You can look now."

Her long lashes flutter open, and the moment her eyes soak in a valley jam-packed with orange wildflowers, her lips stretch into an enormous smile. "How long have they been here?" She swings her eyes over to me.

"I don't know." I shrug. "As long as I can remember they've always been here."

She shifts her eyes back to the native plants. "They just grow freely all by themselves?"

"Yes."

"I've ... I've seen nothing like it before. They're so beautiful. I can't believe what I'm seeing!" She looks at me for a moment before biting down on her bottom lip.

"What?"

"Come on." She rushes off, squealing and racing her way through the flowers. Her long brown hair trails out behind her like a cape.

With one hand shoved in my pocket, I wait there, watching as her hands skim over the tops of the thick, velvety blossoms. The wildflowers wobble back and forth under her mesmerising touch. A moment later, she stops in the middle of the field. And then, as if absorbed in the illusion, she begins to twirl, slowly at first. And, as she picks up the pace, her fingertips tickle the tops of the blossoms.

"Oh, come feel them, Toby! Aren't they glorious?" Her laughter resonates out into the silence, and I can't help but smile.

I peer sideways out across the field, and suddenly it hits me—this pallet of beauty. I take in the bright array of delicate butterflies, the diamond-shaped petals stretching upwards toward the sun, their sweet aroma dancing through the air. It's as if I too am discovering the flowers for the very first time but through her eyes.

Turning my head, I catch Hildy standing there, arms out, head back, soaking up the sun. It's enough to make my breath weaken in my throat. I watch the way the sun streams through the curls of her hair. All the beauty in the world would find it hard to compete with her at this moment. Inside my tranquil bubble, I hear birdsong drift through the air.

Hildy turns her head, then yells. "If I had these flowers anywhere near my house, I would never leave them." She walks on. I race to catch up. "Toby, do you have any idea how incredible this place is?"

"Yeah, I do. I've always known how special it is." I peer over to the left and watch the blossoms ripple in the breeze. "Only a few people know they exist. It's because they're safeguarded behind the tall grass. It's as if God wanted only a few people to witness the beauty." I straighten my shoulders and swivel my head back to find two green eyes studying my profile. Every muscle in my body tightens as I shift from foot to foot. When my nerves finally get the better of me, I bend onto one knee, trace my fingers down the thick fuzzy shaft of a wild-flower, and pluck it clean from the ground. Standing there, I swirl the bloom between my thumb and forefinger. The wind picks up. On impulse, I look up. Hildy's hair lifts in the breeze, and I watch her run her fingers through it as she tries to keep it under control. Above us, the sun dips in behind a cloud, throwing a shadow out over the land. I offer her the flower.

She beams the widest smile as she holds the flower in her hand as if it's a valuable gem. "Thank you." She admires it for the moment, and then pulls it in under her nose, breathing in the delightful scent.

Together, we wander happily through the valley of flowers.

At the end of the track, the land falls off sharply out onto a clearing. From where we stand, there on the top of the rise overlooking the river, we can see out over the ridge and into the distance. Shielding her eyes, Hildy takes in the view. I point out over to the right, across the treetops, to show her the outskirts of town. But it isn't long until our eyes catch something in the water below.

Bill and Sam are down there, splashing and jostling in the water. One minute, Bill's throwing river mud at Sam. And then the next, it's Sam's turn to have a go.

"Is this where you come every day?"

"Yes, this is it." My words come easily. "This is my favourite place. Notice how the water reflects the sky." I point forward.

Her eyes narrow as she follows the water downstream, taking in the alluring snaking curves.

"I don't know why I like it so much," I tell her. "I guess I find it calming. But not after a storm. You should see it—the way the river thrashes in anger. And then the next day the water's all quiet and soothing like everything is forgotten and there's a chance to start over again." I take a deep breath and turn my face towards her. "This may sound silly, but I feel this place calling me." Embarrassed, I look away.

"No, Toby, I don't think that's silly at all." She steps in front of me and stares into my face. "It's obvious this place means a great deal to you. I appreciate you telling me that." She drops her eyes down to her cupped hands in front of her waist. "I think it's lovely that you have somewhere special that means the world to you." She lifts her head. We stand there for the longest time, staring at each other. Her expression is tender. She holds no judgement. I sense the slight rise and fall of her chest as she breathes. The tiny hairs on the back of my neck stand on end.

Suddenly, the noise of Bill and Sam yelling out to each other brings us back from our trance-like state. Hildy tucks her windblown hair behind her ears and turns back to admire the view.

"It's stunning up here, Toby."

"Yeah, it sure is."

Over the next few minutes, we drift down the slope. I am aware of our shoulders touching. As we walk under the tall canopy of trees, I toss my head back to look up as patches of blue sky appear and then disappear through the swaying branches.

When we move out onto the clearing, I feel Hildy's eyes watching me. I quickly glance across. She smiles, and I wonder what she thinks about the environment that has helped shaped me into the person I am today. It's probably lame compared to the exotic world she experiences every day, but it's my world, my place, and no matter what anyone thinks, I will always be proud of it.

I lead her up onto the riverbank, the sand shifting in under our shoes at every step. Directly in front of us, Sam and Bill continue to play their childish game.

"Sam!" I yell. "Come over here and meet Hildy."

They both twist around to the sound of my voice, and I can't help but smile at their mud-stained faces.

Hildy steps around me. "Hello, Sam." She stops short of the water lapping at the front of her shoes. "It's a pleasure to meet you."

Sam's eyes widen and fixate on Hildy. Within seconds, his whole body stiffens, his mouth gapes, and he appears to be frozen with shock. To be totally honest, at this point, I'm not even sure if his heart's still beating.

Behind him, Bill clears his throat and slaps his hand on top of the water, hoping to grab Sam's attention. Sam doesn't move. His eyes stay staring straight at Hildy.

Hildy looks back over her shoulder. "Wow, don't I know how to spoil a party!"

Bill shuffles forward. "Ah ... come on, Sam, you're shaming yourself." With that, he draws in a gulp of air and collapses down under the water. Re-emerging, he hurls a handful of river mud over at Sam.

Splat!

The thick brown paste hits Sam in the throat. It takes a few seconds for his body to melt before his mouth closes. "Just you wait, Bill. You're gonna get it!" He dives under the water in a dolphin-like manner, and when he resurfaces the game goes on.

As Hildy and I remain on the shoreline, I watch her as she takes in the scenery. When a dozen or so screeching white cockatoos charge through the air, she lifts her face up to the heavens. When they move out of view, Hildy tucks the wildflower behind her ear and crouches down to draw in the sand with her finger.

On the surface, Hildy's a wealthy socialite, but the more I get to know her, study her, I can see there's so much more to her than that. Despite our different worlds, there's something about her, something so natural that makes me feel at ease.

Then, suddenly, everything stops.

My insides tighten when Hildy stands and I see the thick layer of mud that now clings to her. It's everywhere—in her hair, over her face, down the front of her dress. Her arms stiffen. Her mouth and eyes shut tightly to stop the muck from seeping in. She's a complete mess.

In front of us, Bill and Sam stand stock still in the water. Each grubby face expresses disbelief. Bill closes his mouth and swallows.

"I'm sorry, Hildy." Bill shakes his head. "I didn't mean it."

My pulse races as I move over to her. "Are you okay?"

She doesn't answer.

I throw a quick side glance to Bill, who seems as anxious as I am. By the time I look back, Hildy's already clawing the gunk away from her eyes. With a quick flick of her wrist, mud drops to the ground. Little by little, her mud-covered lashes flutter open.

In the tense silence, the three of us gawk at her as she peers down to her ruined dress. A second later, she lifts her hand and runs her palm across the front of her frock, smearing the soil deeper into the fabric. After that, she leans over, unbuckles the straps of her shoes, and steps out of them. At this point, she shares a quick glance at me before stepping into the water. She leans forward. The current touches the hem of her dress as she washes her hands.

Out the corner of my eye, I catch Bill and Sam sharing a quick glance.

Then, from out of nowhere, mud splatters over Bill's face, hitting him square on the chin.

Sam's laughter bounces across the water. "Good one, Hildy!"

Hildy's voice, when it comes out, is cheerful. "Now we're even, Bill!" There's a hint of mischief playing in her eyes.

All of a sudden, everything relaxes. It's as if we've all let out a long, exhausting breath. I laugh out loud and view Bill, who, surprisingly, is enjoying himself like the rest of us. It's a shock because he hates being the subject of any joke. He makes a funny face and then ducks under the water. When he resurfaces, he bolts up onto the riverbank and stops in front of me.

Out of habit, I push him away. "Get lost."

In a rushed set of actions, he slaps a handful of river mud down on my head. The thick goo slides its way down over my cheeks. I glance up and take in the satisfaction beaming over his face as the thrill of revenge strokes away at his ego. "Now *we're* even, brother." He turns around, wipes his grotty hands down over his wet thighs, and walks towards Hildy. "Now, shall we try this again? I'm Bill, the idiot you met before."

"Yes." She smiles, accepting his hand. "Hello, Bill."

"I'm real sorry about what I said at the house." He releases his grip. "Well, it's ..." He licks his lips. "We don't get many visitors out here, and you surprised me."

Looking back, I guess that was the moment Bill's opinion about Hildy changed. She was nothing like those other society girls he had encountered over the years. He had seen her fun-loving side. We had all seen that she didn't care if she was covered in mud. Bill and Hildy accepted each other for who they were and not for what they had.

Over time, they grew comfortable with each other. I couldn't see it back then, but I understand now why Bill would also come to fall in love with Hildy.

5

Hours later, as the sun dangles down near the horizon, I reach across and scoop up Hildy's hand as I have one more thing I'd like to show her.

Out of breath, we arrive back at the house and go out to the back verandah where I find my mother already sitting in one of the three rockers. As Hildy goes over to a vacant chair, I turn to take in the vibrant display of red and orange colours splashed across the sky.

"Good, we haven't missed it."

"What haven't we missed?"

"I wanted to show you this before you go." I sit in the chair next to her.

The sky intensifies as the beauty and wonder of the pallet of colour drops further behind the seam of the world.

It's not long before Hildy leans in and whispers. "Toby, what exactly are we doing?"

I look towards her and notice the orange glow of light spilling over the contours of her face. She is a work of art. "We're watching the sunset."

She shifts in the chair. "I'm sorry, but I don't understand."

"I was five years old when my grandmother died."

"I'm sorry."

"I'd never experienced someone dying before. And I didn't understand how someone could be here one minute and then gone the next. Bill and I cried for hours. I don't think he understood it either. So my mother brought us out here and sat us down in these same chairs." As I speak, her eyes never leave my face. "She told us to look out at the sky and wait for the moment when day and night linger together on the horizon. For when that moment happens, the sky will split in two. That's when you get a glimpse into heaven and a chance to say hello to all those who have gone there." Hildy's eyes drift back to the sky. "Mum and I sit out here every evening, and sometimes Bill joins us, just to say hello."

With her face turned to the colourful display, she smiles softly. I remain quiet, giving her time to stay lost in the moment. "You're different." She looks across at me, then down to her cupped hands folded in her lap. "So different to the boys I associate with back in town. I don't think I've ever met anyone like you before."

I tuck my legs in under my chair. "Is that a good thing?"

"Yes." She laughs and then stretches her legs out in front of her, crossing them over at the ankles. "Trust me. It's a good thing."

"I gather you've decided about me then."

"Yes, but if you want me to be honest, I'd already decided earlier in town."

I smile. And together, in some unspoken agreement, we shift our faces back and watch the last of the light drain from the sky. Into the peacefulness, we hear the sounds of crickets singing as they beckon to the moon.

Nightfall shifts in quickly, bringing with it a welcome coolness to the land. Somewhere in the distance, an owl hoots as if summoning all nocturnal creatures to come out and play. The moonlight spills, and a canopy of stars materialises. From inside the house, there is movement. Bill's opening and closing the cupboard doors. A few seconds later, after the back door slams, Bill appears at my side.

"So, brother, when are we going to eat?"

I stand quickly. I've been so preoccupied with Hildy, I'd forgotten all about dinner.

"You forgot, didn't you?"

"Yeah. I'm sorry."

Hildy stands, all eyes turn toward her. "Well, it's been lovely meeting you all, but I have to go." She pushes her hair back over her shoulder. "Thank you, Hazel, for the sewing lesson, and Bill ... thank you for the mud pack. I've had such a wonderful time." She gives one last smile before crossing the verandah.

Desperately wanting to go with Hildy, I throw a sharp look over at Bill.

"Go. It's fine. I'll try to cook something."

Even before he finishes the sentence, I'm on my way. "Hildy, wait! I'll walk you home."

She slows and turns around. "Are you sure? What about your dinner?"

"Nah, it'll be fine. Bill's going to do it."

We make our way back through the house and out onto the front porch. As we walk down the steps, I peer out into the night and take in the jagged flashes of lightning flickering somewhere in the distance. There is a storm brewing.

Down along the driveway, our footsteps move in perfect time. The only sound resonating out into the mild night air is the gravel crunching under our feet.

"Thanks for allowing me time with your family today." She turns to look at me. "I've had such a wonderful time getting to know all of you."

"It's not a problem, and you're welcome back anytime."

"I might just take you up on that." She threads her arm through mine, and my pulse quickens. "I like your mum. She's adorable. The two of you are so lucky to have such a caring mother." She tosses her head back to look at the stars. I follow her gaze. "The three of you seem to have an exceptional bond."

"Yeah, my mum has done so much for us over the years. Even now, with all the struggles, she still manages to teach us what's important in life." I lower my head and see two more lightning bolts breaking through the darkness. The sky is awakening.

"Well, I think it's adorable the way you two are with her. I only wish I had that kind of relationship with either one of my parents, but I don't." She pauses for a moment, and when she continues, there's a different pitch in her voice. "I guess that's something that I'll never have."

"What about your sister?"

"Who, Bea?" She twists her head and looks directly at me. "No. Bea's always trying to get our father's approval. So, she tells him anything to get me into trouble."

"Will you get into trouble for ruining your dress?"

"No. They won't know about that. If anything, I'm sure Bea's already told my father that I accepted a drink from you. She can't help herself. They won't say anything until breakfast tomorrow. Right now, my father will be in the parlour drinking his whiskey. Mother will be busy planning her next high tea or social gathering. They are both so predictable." She lets out a long breath. "My family is different to yours, Toby. We don't show affection in the same way."

"I wouldn't say Bill shows me any affection."

"Not openly, no, but deep down it's clear that he cares about you."

"Maybe your family is the same. They just don't know how to say it."

Another flash of lightning illuminated the sky, this one followed by a faint rumble of thunder.

"No, that's not it. Because I remember when I was four years of age, I told my mother I loved her."

"See? Told ya it's just a different way."

"No, it's not, Toby, because she looked right at me after I said it. But she said nothing back. Instead, she got up and left the room." She shrugs and stares down the street into the darkness. "From that day on, I've never been able to say it to anyone."

"Well, maybe your mother didn't hear you?"

"No, she heard me. She doesn't care about those sorts of things." She blinks back a tear and rests the side of her face against my arm.

Soft rain begins to fall.

"Only certain things matter to people when they have money," she says. "It's all about how much they have and how they can show it off to others in their social rank. I've seen it. It makes not one of them happy. My parents are the same. Sometimes they can't stand to be in the same room with each other. But to everyone else, they portray this happy, loving couple. It's all an act. All of it." As we round the corner, she lifts her head off my arm. "Anyway, enough of that talk. Tell me, how do you put up with the rumours when clearly they're not true?"

"I don't worry about it. But Bill has a hard time dealing with it. He gets so worked up sometimes that he feels the need to defend our mum."

"You don't feel the need to tell everyone they're wrong about her and about you and Bill?"

"No. It won't change the way they think about us, so why bother?" I bite my lip and pause for a few seconds before continuing. "One thing I do know—it's challenging. But what can I do about it? I have a job. I have a family, and today I made a new friend, so it can't all be bad now can it?"

"Yes, that's true. You do have a job. You also have a family." She smiles and squeezes my arm. "I'm only teasing you, Toby. Yes, you have made a new friend today, and so have I. Do you want to know what I think? I think that, if people took the time to get to know your family, then they might feel differently about all of you." She hesitates for a second as if thinking of something else. "You should look at it as their loss and not yours." She stops and takes back her hand. "Well, this is me."

I turn my head and peer past two large stone pillars down the length of a long drive to the lights of what looks like a three-storey building.

"Can I ask why you didn't ask me to dance last night?"

I look back to Hildy. "Why? What would you have said if I did?"

"I would have said yes of course." She pushes her damp hair away from her eyes.

"You would have? Even though everyone would have looked at us?"

"Yes. I don't care what they would have thought. I wanted to dance with you. I thought I made that obvious."

"But what about the boy you were dancing with?"

"Who?" Her brows furrow. "Oh, you mean John?" She drops her head back and laughs. "No. It's not like that at all. He's just a brother to one of the girls I know. He's so annoying, always going on about how he's going to be a banker when he finishes school."

"Well, in that case, would you like to dance?" I hold my palm up as if leading her out onto the dance floor.

"What? Here?" She glances back over her shoulder. "But it's raining."

"Yes, I know it's raining."

"There's no music."

"It doesn't matter about the music."

"It seems foolish, Toby. I mean, I will feel silly."

"Come on. Just give it a try. If you don't like it, then I promise we can stop." I step in closer so that our eyes are almost level. "Relax. Just go with the moment."

"Okay." She lets out a long breath.

As we come together, I guide my hand carefully behind her back. She looks up and inhales sharply.

"Are you okay?" I ask.

"Yes. Yes, I'm fine." She nods.

With the storm moving around us, we sway back and forth to our own silent tune. The idea of her body so close to mine and the smell of wildflowers still playing over her wet skin seduces all my senses. Suddenly, every tense muscle in Hildy's body seems to relax as she loses herself in the moment. She closes her eyes. Now I can gaze freely at her beautiful face. I watch the way the water trickles down over her smooth ivory skin as if it were silk. I fight the temptation to lean forward to taste those warm, cherry lips. Slowly, her eyes flutter open. Small droplets of rain cling to her long lashes. Her breath quickens, and so does mine. Finally, I give in to temptation when she leans forward, allowing herself to be kissed. The taste of her rain-soaked lips makes the world fall away. The moment is ours.

From out of nowhere, a roar of thunder explodes overhead, splitting the two of us apart. The rain falls more heavily now, drenching our skin.

"I'm sorry, but I have to go." Hildy turns away and races through the gateway.

"Wait!" I step forward. "When will I see you again?"

She stops and takes her time. I sense her slight embarrassment. "Tomorrow. I will see you again tomorrow, Toby."

"When tomorrow?" I yell out into the rain.

She spins around and walks in reverse down the drive. "Don't you worry. I shall find you tomorrow." She smiles and turns back around.

I settle there, watching her skip down the drive until I lose sight of her in the shadows.

Eighteen

6

She had ignited my life like the sun. Nine months. That's all it has taken—nine months to infuse herself into my soul. She came back to the house the very next day, and has come back every day after that.

I know when I get home from work Hildy will be sitting in the kitchen sewing a patchwork quilt with my mother, who also has grown fond of Hildy. Most days, my mother has the needle threaded ready for her arrival. And on those days when my mother's memory abandons her, Hildy re-introduces herself, sits down at the table, and starts up a conversation.

As for Bill, he seems more composed with Hildy around. Their newfound friendship only grows stronger with each passing day. He trusts her, and that is something he finds hard to do outside our family. Many times I catch the two of them joining forces to share a "one-up" moment on Sam and me.

Together, they are hilarious, and often I find I'm laughing at their natural banter.

Sometimes I forget what my life was like before Hildy. It's as if she's always been a part of the pack. During our time together, I've taught her how to skim stones over the water. It's one of her favourite things, other than the wildflowers of course. She still races through them every day, and as usual, I stand there watching her with complete admiration.

When our day winds down, we all sit out on the back verandah and watch the sky split. Then, it's on to my favourite time of the night when I get to walk her home. That's when we share our deepest secrets and when I get to taste those warm, cherry lips again. My life is perfect.

Then in one split moment, everything changes.

It is like any regular afternoon down at the river. Bill and Sam stand waist deep in the murky water, wrestling, challenging each other to see which one is the weaker. While they play their silly game, Hildy and I sit talking in our usual spot under the shade of the old ghost gums.

"Oh, did I mention that Bea has a boyfriend?" She stretches her legs out in front.

"No." I pull a piece of stalky grass and place it between my teeth.

"It's a boy my parents approve of and—"

Her chatter evaporates when Bill lets out a yelp, followed by a loud expletive. Our eyes shift down to the river.

"Something bit me! Something bit me!" He thrashes through the water and then races up onto the riverbank, the sand clinging to his feet. "Shit! Shit!" Stopping a few feet in front of us, he yanks open the waistband of his shorts and peers down into them. "Shit! It's stinging!" He tosses a quick look back at Sam, who is now trudging through the water.

56

"Gosh, Bill. Do you have to do that right there?" Hildy shields her eyes and turns her head away.

Sam pauses when he arrives at Bill's side. As he sets his wet hands down on his hips, the corners of his mouth fight hard not to smile. "So ... um ... tell me Bill, is it still there or did something chew it off?"

An explosion of laughter ripples out across the peaceful land, which soon dissolves under Bill's fierce glare.

Biting down on my bottom lip, I cast a look over at Hildy, who has her head down resting on her knees. Her shoulders shake with silent laughter. I look away before the amusement spreads.

Bill snaps the elastic back to his waist and glares over at Sam. "It's not funny, you know."

"Oh, but it is."

Another ripple of laughter adds only more anger to an already bubbling situation. With his fists clenched at his sides, Bill's knuckles turn white. "You're such a dick, Sam." He turns and marches off across the sand and snatches his shirt up off the ground. "And so are you, brother." He swings around and makes his way to the house.

With all eyes on him, he reaches the top of the rise, and just when we think he's about to disappear down the other side, he stops, turns, and gives us the finger.

The chuckles roar out of our mouths; we cannot stop. Fat tears accumulate and spill, racing down over our cheeks. We're laughing so much, our breaths strain, our ribs ache.

Finally, after a good twenty minutes, we manage to get the hilarity under control.

"Well, I'd better go check on him." Sam collects his shirt from the ground and slips his head through, followed by both arms. "Just to make sure his ego's still intact."

"Yeah, he got pretty annoyed with us." I laugh out loud again.

"Yeah, but don't worry about it. Remember, he's got that stinging thing he has to attend to." He turns his head and looks at the rise. "Well, I'll see you two up there."

I lean into Hildy, wrap my arm around her, and bless the side of her face with my kisses. "You look beautiful today."

She gives the faintest of smiles. "You say that every day."

"Cause, every day it's true."

A strand of hair flops down over her eyes, and with a quick glide of her fingers, she shoves it away. "Are you coming down to the water?" She stands and brushes the loose grass from the back of her dress.

"Nah, just give me a minute." Resting back on my elbow, I stretch my legs out in front. "I'll be over there soon."

I lift my face to soak up the sun, and I breathe in the air rich with the smell of eucalyptus.

Over on the shoreline, Hildy crouches and scratches through the sand as if considering which pebble to use. Then, when she stands, she flicks her wrist. The stone dances across the water. A moment later, she's back searching for another pebble.

I close my eyes and pick up every sound— the frogs, the birds, the stones skimming over the water. This place is perfection. I open my eyes and watch the light breeze play freely through Hildy's wild mane.

Out the corner of my eye, I detect movement. I sit up, use my hand to shield my eyes from the glaring sun, and look to the cluster of gums on my left.

There, a middle-aged man emerges out of the trees. I run my eyes down over this drifter, taking in his scruffy hair, his overgrown beard, and his filthy clothes. When his eyes fall on Hildy, he stops and pulls the swag off his shoulder, lowering it down onto the sand.

All my senses scream out at me. I stand and throw a quick look up to the rise, but it's too late. Sam's already disappeared down the other side. I glance back. Fear rockets through my body when I notice him standing only a few yards away from Hildy. She hasn't seen him yet; she's too busy fossicking for pebbles in the thick river sand.

I step forward and then suddenly freeze as the stranger's head turns and looks over at me. The silence hangs. His wolflike eyes examine every inch of my body. Swallowing, I come to realise my sticklike figure is no threat to his thick, sturdy frame. Dry-mouthed, I step forward and somehow manage to keep my voice calm. "Hildy."

She stands and tosses her wavy hair back over her shoulder. The moment her eyes soak in the stranger, her smile dissolves. Her whole body stiffens.

I push my body between Hildy and the stranger. Now I'm standing only inches away from him. The smell of rotten teeth and body odour is almost enough to make me vomit. Hildy presses in against my back. I reach behind to locate her hand.

"Get out of the way, boy."

"We were just going, anyway. But you're welcome to stay." I step across to the right, Hildy moves in time with me.

"No, you're not." With no warning, he steps forward, blocking the way.

Glancing up, I stare straight at him, but it's difficult to make eye contact while he centres his attention on Hildy. I don't like the way his eyes suggest things, things he shouldn't be thinking.

The seconds tick by.

My heart pounds harder in my chest; it's about to explode. The sweat oozes out of my skin. "We really must go. My big brother will be here any second looking for us." I step again to the right.

He mirrors my actions and obstructs the way. "So, what ya gonna do now, boy?" He tilts his head to one side, mocking me with a grin, wide enough to expose three blackened teeth.

"Oh god, Toby," Hildy murmurs into my back.

The fear of the situation rests in my brain, slowing down the process to find a solution. If I say the right thing, do the right thing, then Hildy will be okay. Fail, and she will pay the ultimate price. My one priority is to get her out of here away from him. I will take the consequences. An idea pops into my head. She can run. He'll be slow. I release her hand and scream out as loud as I can in case Sam is still close enough to hear. "Go now, Hildy! Get Bill or get Sam. Don't you stop for anything!"

Her feet slip as she bursts out from my side. With one mighty leap, I plunge my body into the intruder. But the moment I make contact, his large hands seize hold of my shoulders, tossing me sideways onto the ground. Adrenalin pumping, I scramble onto all fours, knowing I have to get back up on my feet. I get one leg up, and just when I'm about to get up on the other, his boot pounds hard in against my side. The sheer force of it knocks me face down on the ground. I try to suck in the air, but it's thick ... thick like soup.

"Call her back now." He leans over the top of me.

"No!" My breath comes out in spurts. I force my body up onto my knees to see Hildy bolting to the rise. Good, she's gonna make it. She's gonna be safe.

"I said call her back."

When I don't comply, he lashes out and ploughs his boot into the middle of my back. I fall forward. The right side of my face settles on the sand. My first instinct is to stand, but the paralysing pain keeps me down. My lungs billow. With every uneven breath, I feel as if a knife is pushing into my flesh. He walks around me. I attempt to move, but it's too late. His boot presses firmly in on the back of my neck. Every second the pressure builds, and I have to bite down on my bottom lip to stop from screaming out. Every muscle in my body tenses. The pain is too much. A blood-curdling scream arises from my throat. I have to let it out.

From where I'm pinned down, I watch Hildy's pace decelerate the moment my scream catches her. She stops and turns. Her whole face crumbles. "Leave him alone!" There's panic in her voice.

"Come here, or I'll hurt him."

"No!" I try to yell, but the pressure on my throat only produces a sickening groan.

In the grip of soundless panic, Hildy scans the rise.

I twist and convulse under his boot like a wild animal trying to elude a trap. But he presses down harder. I let out a raw howl. Every hair on my body stands on end. Slowly, I give up the fight. Now all I can do is lie here, listen, and wait for the sound of my neck to snap.

From across the clearing, Hildy's voice yells. "What are you doing?" A choked cry bursts out of her. "Please, please stop. I beg of you. Please don't hurt him."

"Do you know what you have to do?"

"Yes." Her chin quivers in a harsh sob. "I won't go. I will stay here." Her legs collapse underneath her. She falls to the ground. "Just don't hurt him, please."

The second his boot releases my neck the will to fight surges back into me. I get up on my feet, ignoring the broken rib screaming out at me. Every one of my tired muscles pushes me forward.

When Hildy registers I'm up on my feet, she stands quickly and wipes the tears from her face.

I race to catch up to the intruder, but the second I come near him, he spins around and strikes the side of my face. It's bone jarring. I collapse on the ground. My breath stalls. Through the blurriness, I see him towering over me. He draws back his fist and punches my jaw. The blood pools on the side of my mouth. Every repeated blow brings white-hot agony. My body gives up the fight. Everything slows. Just before the darkness closes in on me, I hear Hildy scream out one last time.

7

A familiar voice touches the edges of my mind. It's getting stronger and louder, clearer with every repetition. How strange it is to hear such intensity in Bill's voice. I try fluttering my eyes open, but the blackness swallows me once again.

Then I hear Bill's voice calling to me again. Slowly, the darkness retreats. I am drifting. I try to open my eyes, but only one of them seems to work. As I lie here, I become aware of where I am—the clouds overhead, the sand underneath, the sound of the river. I half wonder if I'm dreaming.

Suddenly, Bill leans over, blocking my view of the sky. "Toby, can you hear me?"

The pain rockets through my chest, throat, and face. I let out an agonising scream as Bill continues to talk. But the torturous pain hijacks my ability to hear what he's saying. I struggle to achieve a comfortable position. Every movement makes me hiss with distress.

"Brother, you need to stay still. Look at me." He shoves both hands on my shoulders, securing me into place. "Breathe. You need to breathe."

I quiet my mind and push myself into a place I can handle, ignoring the fact that my one working eye is clogged with shadowed specks. I continue to blink until Bill's face comes into focus.

"Jesus, Toby, what the hell happened here?"

Blood roams through my mouth. The tension shows on my face as I try to patch my memory together. I lift my hand up to my eye. It's swollen shut. Then, everything snaps into place. "Hildy. Where's Hildy?"

Bill takes in a deep breath and slowly releases it. I realise he's stalling.

The thoughts accumulate in my head. They are no longer rational. "Damn it, Bill, just tell me where she is." I push up onto my elbow. The brutal blast cuts right through my ribcage, pressing me back down.

"She's over there." I hear unfamiliar shaking in his voice. "It's bad, brother. Real bad."

"Get me up."

"Just wait a minute, will ya?" He looks me straight in the eye. "You need to know something first."

"What'd he do to her?"

He takes a ragged breath. "She is severely beaten, and it looks like she's been ..." He can't complete the sentence. Instead, he swallows.

His words splinter right through me. My heart constricts. My stomach tightens. I now feel sick.

"Hildy has her eyes open, but it's as if she's not there."

I stare up at his red-rimmed eyes.

"No matter what I do, I can't bring her round. And—"

"And what?"

"Her dress has been ripped from her body."

"Well, get something to cover her." Tears ooze out the sides of my eyes. "She needs to be covered."

"I've already done it." He lifts his chin and stares out into the distance. "I've covered her with my shirt."

My eyes drop to his naked chest, not knowing why I hadn't noticed it earlier. "Just get me up."

Bill slips both hands in under my elbows and shifts me onto my feet. A raw animalistic scream vibrates out of me. Everything hurts. My body struggles to stay upright.

"Are you okay?" Bill clutches my arms, holding most of my body weight.

I take slow, shallow breaths until the pain finally ebbs.

"Come," says Bill, breaking the silence. "See if you can bring Hildy round."

I lift my head, and time suddenly stops. Everything rushes backward away from me as I view her lifeless body slumped on the ground. It's a blow to my heart, and I feel myself stagger.

"Hey." Bill collects me before I fall.

The image of Hildy collapsing on the ground plays back through my mind. Into the silence, there's a crow cawing somewhere in the distance, trees rustling their leaves in the breeze. All around me, life continues on as usual, but mine has abruptly stopped. Every expelled breath now controls the grief threatening to consume my body. He just left her there, broken and battered, discarded as if she is nothing.

"Did you hear me?" Bill releases his hands from under my elbows and straightens up.

"What?"

"I said, if you can't get her to come round, then I'll race over to Picker's and get him to get the doctor."

Bill helps me, and we move across the clearing. Every step exposes another snapshot of her battered body. The imprint is unimaginable. It's the horror that takes hold of your emotions, that the one person you care for most in this world should be maltreated. As Hildy lies there so helpless, so lifeless, so withdrawn, it becomes clear what she has suffered. It's the sight of the prominent bruises scattered across her face, her torn upper lip, which is still weeping, blood that lies in unseen places underneath Bill's shirt. Tears flood my eyes. I refuse to let my legs go weak under the invisible guilt that sits on my shoulders. "I couldn't stop him, Bill."

"You can't think of that now." He leans forward to steal a glance at my face. "Hildy needs us now more than ever."

"I don't think I can do it."

"But you have to." He steps in front of me. "What she's gone through is so unthinkable. She needs us—both of us—to help her get through it. I'd do it by myself, brother, but I've already tried. Listen, I promise, if you can get her to come round, I'll take care of everything. Do you think you can do that? "

I nod. It's all I can do to hold back the pain of seeing her this way.

Bill helps me down beside her. On folded knees, I lean over Hildy. Her eyes are frozen over, staring upwards, looking at the sky. "Hildy, can you hear me?"

I wait a few seconds. She doesn't respond.

"Try again." Bill touches my shoulder. There's desperation in his voice.

"Please, Hildy." I lift my hand, gently stroking the side of her face. I try to reach into her, to let her know it's safe to come back now.

66

Through the silence, a muffling sound resonates out through her broken lips.

"Oh, thank god," I hear Bill say from behind.

"Good. That's it, Hildy."

She closes her eyes and shifts her hand up to touch the right side of her face, but the moment her fingers come into contact with her cheek, she winces.

It's gut wrenching to see her in so much pain. In some way, I wonder if the simple fact that she knows me and was here with me has caused this damage. How in the hell am I ever going to say sorry for any of this?

"Toby, are you okay?" Her voice is croaky.

"Yes, yes. I'm fine. Don't you worry about me." I release a shuddering breath, lean over, and plant a kiss on her forehead. The taste of blood plays on my lips. "Don't talk. You need to save your energy."

I rock back on my heels. Bill leans forward and whispers in my ear. "Pull yourself together, brother."

Not making sense of what he's saying, I glance up. Only then I discover the tears dribbling down over my face. I don't precisely recall when they first appeared. I need to be strong for Hildy. I will allow the tears to come later. Swiftly, I swipe them away. Hildy reaches up for my hand, and I let her take it. Under my fingers, I feel her broken nails. There's evidence she fought back.

"Bill's gonna carry you back to the house." I manage to add with a forced smile.

She nods and licks her bottom lip, flinching the second her tongue catches her open wound.

From behind, Bill steps forward and takes charge. "Come on. Let's get you up so I can get Hildy up to the house." He holds out his hand. I grab it for support.

As he pulls me up, the unbearable pain slices through my

ribcage. I want to scream out, but somehow I manage to hold it in for Hildy's sake. "You make sure you're careful with her, you hear me?" I say through gritted teeth, trying to control the pain.

"I will." He gives my arm a tiny squeeze. "You have my word, brother. She is important to me too, you know. Are you gonna be able to make it back up to the house?"

"Yes," I snap. Somehow his question makes me feel slightly weaker than I already feel. Retreating, I shove my hands into my pockets and watch Bill lower himself down beside Hildy.

He picks up a clump of bloody hair that's stuck to the side of her face and sets it back into her tangled mane. "Hildy, you're gonna have to put my shirt on. Your dress has been torn."

"Yes. I remember him doing that."

I close my eyes. Every word punctures my heart.

"Now, do you think you're able to sit up?"

"I'm not sure."

"I can help you. I promise I won't look. Trust me. You have my word."

"Okay, but be careful because it hurts."

While Hildy gets ready, lifting her hand up to her chest, securing the shirt into place, Bill slips his arm in under her back.

"All right, we'll do this on the count of three. Ready? One, two, and three." His voice is softer, gentler than usual.

As Bill lifts Hildy into a sitting position, she lets out a loud groan.

"Did I hurt you?" Bill asks, leaving his hand in behind her back, steadying her.

"No. It's tender. That's all." She lifts her face. I regard the dark bruises around her throat. Five, in fact—long and lean and in the shape of fingers.

68

As I stand there watching, the guilt devours me. In my mind, I am conscious that Bill would have been able to protect her. He's definitely powerful enough. Now all I can do is stand here and watch him help her because I'm too useless to do anything. Because of me, there is no way back to our existence as those carefree kids we were only hours ago. Our innocence has been taken.

Hildy glances up. Her eyes cling to mine. The pain is evident on her face. Suddenly seeming like an intruder, I have to turn away to offer some privacy.

Behind me, Bill dresses Hildy blindly into his shirt. As I stand there waiting, a wave of heat surges through my body. Quickly, I push back any notion that I need to sit, for doing so will only show weakness. It's a trait I've already exposed too many times today.

"You can open your eyes now, Bill," says Hildy.

I spin around. My emotions are all over the place. More insecurities surface as I watch Bill push her hair back away from her face.

"I'm sorry, Hild, but this is gonna hurt." With that, he pushes his strong, muscular arms in under her and scoops her up from the ground. She nuzzles her face in against his bare chest, and I watch them whoosh past me.

By the time I've travelled a few paces, Bill's already vanished down the other side of the rise. Now I am left alone.

Each passing step plays out the events of the last few hours. They replay over and over as if from a spool of film in my head. I wonder what I could have done differently.

As soon as I reach the wildflowers, I stop to catch my breath. Leaning forward, I rest my hands down on my knees and take slow, shallow puffs. Hildy's battered face flashes before my eyes, and I think about the hysteria she must have felt when I was just lying there, unable to help her. From out of the depths of my body, all the guilt races up. It drowns me. In my emotional state, I collapse onto my knees and bury my swollen face in my hands. The sobs tumble out of me. The pain flares through my chest. But I don't care, for every ounce of me deserves to be punished for not keeping her safe. I scream out again and again just to punish myself some more. The tears continue to flow out of me like water from a dam. I drop onto my back as tiny whimpers race up and seal off my throat. Now I start to panic. I close my eye, trying to regulate my breathing, I take shallow quivering breaths.

Sometime later, when my pulse slows, I pop open my one good eye and stare up at the darkening sky. All around me, I hear the crickets call for the moon. This place, the place I love so dearly, will no longer hold a soft spot in my heart. It will now forever haunt my soul.

"There you are."

Bill's voice jerks me back into the moment. I sniff. Turning my head away from him, I wipe the wetness from my face. "I thought you were going to get the doctor."

"I was, but Hildy won't let me." He moves in closer.

"Where is she?" I try to mask the emotion in my voice, but it's no use. I sniffle.

"She's up in the bathroom." He kneels down and looks into my face. "She's asking for you."

"How can I face her, Bill, after ... after everything that's happened?"

"You just have too."

"How is she?"

"Come on. Let's get you up to the house, and you can see for yourself." He slips his hands in under my shoulder.

"Wait, Bill."

He stops and peers down at me.

I stare up at him for the longest time wanting to say so much but not knowing how to say the words.

"I know, brother." He looks away and then helps me up onto my feet.

8

I've been standing outside the bathroom door for a while now, trying to find the courage to enter the room. I close my eyes to gather my thoughts. *You can do this. You can be strong for her.* I open my eyes, and before I can change my mind once again, I lift my hand and tap my knuckles against the door.

"Hildy, can I come in?"

I wait a moment. She doesn't answer. I knock again and push open the door. There, in the dim light, I find her sitting on the floor, leaning against the bathtub, staring down at the floorboards, lost somewhere inaccessible.

I step into the room and latch the door behind me. Still, Hildy doesn't move.

"Hey," I add softly.

She slowly lifts her head up to the sound of my voice. The new landscape of swollen features registers in my mind.

"Why did he do this to us?"

How can I answer that? A brief silence hangs in the room, which only prolongs the suffering. It is one that I will remember for the rest of my life. I sit down on the floor next to her.

"I don't know why he did it. I'm so sorry."

She pulls her knees up. As she glances sideways, her whole face crumples. I enclose her in my arms as harsh sobs rack through her body. Her tears fall and seep into my shirt, dissolving onto my skin.

No one will ever understand the suffering, or what effect that man's fingerprints will have on the rest of our lives. As I sit there, stroking her hair, rocking her, something within me shuts down. The tears fill my eyes as my composure gives way. The air around us stills as we grieve together in our own little cocoon.

For the longest time, I simply hold her, hoping somehow my arms will absorb all her pain and erase all the blame I feel. Time is no longer relevant as we cling together in our timeless embrace. To what end is she suffering? What support will she need to help fight the storm within?

She pulls back from me and looks through misty eyes. "Are you okay? Oh, Toby, look what he's done to your face."

When I look down at her, a painful jolt passes right through me. I cup the sides of her face with my hands, gently wiping the tears away with my thumbs. A second later, I lean in, gently kissing her cheeks where her salty tears still run.

At some point, I manage to pull myself together and get up on my feet. From out of the top cupboard, I collect a clean facecloth and wet it under the tap. After wringing it out, I neatly fold it over in my hands and return to Hildy. Sitting down, I flinch as the pain drills into my side.

"Are you sure you're okay?"

"Yes. Yes, I'm fine," I lie. I lift the washer up to touch her face, letting the fresh water penetrate her skin. Her eyes never leave mine as I dab her face. I work slowly, softly, down over her swollen cheek, over the ruptured purple bruises across her jawline. The sticky blood comes away. I begin to wonder if she can sense my vulnerability.

On impulse, I lower my head and take my time folding the fabric over in my hand, not knowing what to say to her. My words will never be enough.

After a brief pause, I summon up the strength to work on the other side of her face. I clean the gash in under her eye, and as soon as the washer touches her broken lip, she flinches and clutches at my hand.

The unbearable silence lingers, during which our eyes hold.

"I'm so sorry, Hildy."

"What are you sorry for?" She reaches out and takes the washcloth from my hand and starts cleaning the blood from the edges of my mouth.

"I'm so sorry that I couldn't stop him."

She stops and lowers the washcloth down to her lap. Her eyes look at me with such sadness. "No, Toby, it's not your fault. Please don't think that."

My eyes shift away from her as they become filled with tears.

"Listen to me," she continues. "There was nothing you could have done differently. You did everything to stop him. I saw that. We didn't have a chance out there today."

The sigh that passes out of my mouth is slow. It's as if I expected hearing those words from her mouth would somehow expunge all the blame, but it doesn't. The guilt still festers within me. My eyes drift back slowly, taking in Bill's shirt hanging loosely around her shoulders.

"Here, let me get you one of mum's dresses." I stand.

"No." She points over to the end of the bath. "Bill's already fetched one."

"Of course, he has," I whisper.

For the first time since knowing her, there's unfamiliar awkwardness hovering between us. My eyes, for some reason, can no longer look at her, so I glance around the room. "Well ... I'll let you get dressed." I take a deep breath.

Just when I'm about to step away, she reaches out and takes my hand.

"Toby, wait." First, she gazes at our joined hands, and then her eyes make their way up to my face. She opens her mouth to speak but hesitates and then says nothing. She closes her mouth and releases my hand.

"You know I love you," I say. I force a smile.

She nods and lets her head drop down towards her chest.

I turn and move across to the door.

The aroma of burnt toast wafts down the hall. When I enter the kitchen, I find Bill washing the dishes. He stops rinsing the bowl and turns, his gaze is steady. I remain silent as I make my way to the table.

By the time I settle myself down in one of the chairs, Bill's patience has got the better of him.

He folds his arms up over his chest and leans his hip against the sink. "Well, is Hildy okay?" He raises his brows.

I am aware at some point I will have to answer, but for now, my stubborn pride prevents me from doing so. Instead, I allow my ego to take over. It's the first time I've been in charge of anything over the last few hours.

Bill tosses his arms out in exasperation. "So are you going to answer me or just be an arse?"

"What?"

"I asked about Hildy. Is she okay?"

"She's getting dressed. She'll be out soon." I shift in the chair. "Then you can ask her yourself."

"Why are you like this?" He shakes his head and glares. "Look, I know you're hurting. I can see that, but I'm worried about her too." He catches his breath and slowly blows it out through his cheeks. "She's a bloody mess, brother."

"And you don't think I already know that?" My jaw starts to tick as I glare at him. "Go on, say what you're thinking."

"And what am I supposed to be thinking?"

"That I couldn't protect her."

"And why would I think that for god's sake?"

"Because it's true! Go on, say it!" Tears well in my eyes.

He steps forward and wipes his wet hands down the sides of his pants. "Look at your face. I can see you did everything to stop him. Hell, I don't even know if I could have stopped him. But I'll tell you something right now. When I find him, I'm gonna kill him. That's a promise I make to you and to her."

His words leave a muted silence between us, broken only by the sound of the bathroom door opening. Hildy appears in the doorway. Our faces turn toward her.

Hildy's eyes flicker between the two of us then settle on the floor in front. "I have to go."

"I'll walk you home." I stand and walk across the room.

"Wait," Bill yells from behind. "I'm coming."

I spin around. "Why?"

"Because I want too, that's why."

"But I don't see why you have to come. I can do this on my own you know."

"Brother, I don't care what you say. I'm coming."

"Whatever." I shrug, venting my annoyance at him as he takes control once again.

I walk with Hildy back through the house. When we arrive at the front entrance, I hold open the screen door allowing Hildy to go out. After I step through, I purposely let go of the door. It slams hard into Bill.

"Smart ass," he mumbles, pushing open the door.

Outside, the moon is higher than it generally is when I walk Hildy home. It's late, and the autumn mist is already rolling in. There's also a hint of wood smoke lingering in the night air.

As we walk, I collect Hildy's hand. She remains quiet, her eyes focused on the road ahead. We've both wandered this track so many times, shared our most private thoughts and secrets, and plans for the future, but tonight it's different. I no longer feel as if we're part of the backdrop for the moon and the stars.

9

After what seems to take us forever, we finally arrive out in front of Hildy's place. As we stand there, I catch sight of Bill glancing down the lengthy drive. No doubt he's taking in the surroundings—the towering pillars, the three-storey house. It's a timely reminder of the life Hildy's been born into. Over time, I'm sure he has forgotten. To him, she is just Hildy, the girl who visits our home, who sits and sews with our mother, who enjoys laughing and sharing his practical jokes. I haven't forgotten. I am reminded of it every day when I walk her home. Many times, when she disappears into the shadows of the drive, I wonder what people would think if they knew how much time we spend together.

"Well, thanks for walking me home." Hildy's voice rises to an uncomfortable pitch. "Goodnight." She turns and makes way for the gate.

"Hildy," I yell out, stepping forward. "I have to go with you and tell your parents what happened today."

She turns around, shaking her head. "No! No! You can't. I will tell them later, much later. Please, Toby, don't tell them tonight. My parents have no idea that I go to your house every day." Her voice breaks. "They don't see you the way I see you."

"I know. It doesn't matter what they say. I've heard it all before." I give a forced smile, hoping to lighten the mood. "Besides, if we need any help, we've always got ugly over here." I glance sideways at Bill.

Hildy's eyes shift in the same direction.

"Yep." Bill nods, shoving his hands into his pockets. "It's true. I'm here if you need me. But the ugly part ... I think that jobs already filled, isn't it, brother?" He grins.

Hildy laughs and then straight away flinches. "Oh, Bill, don't make me laugh." She dabs the tips of her fingers over her torn lip.

"I'm sorry, but I agree with Toby on this one. You can't do this by yourself." He rests his hand down on her arm. "I promise we will not leave until everything is sorted out and your parents understand what's happened."

"But they're not aware that I have anything to do with you and Toby. They'll flip when they find out." She turns her head and glances down the driveway as if wondering how long before she can get away from us.

"Hey," Bill says, rubbing her arm.

She turns her attention back to him.

"It doesn't matter what they say about us. Toby and I will be fine. What matters at the moment is you."

She glances back down the drive.

Bill takes her hand in his. "Hild, it will be okay."

She sighs and remains silent as if judging the words carefully in her head. "All right, but please understand it won't be pleasant." She takes a gulp of air before turning around.

Bill and I share a quick glance before joining her. All together, we walk down the length of the drive in silence and step out onto a paved path that runs beneath dozens of trellises heavy with overhanging wisteria. Then, it's over to a series of steps—ten to be exact—that lead up to oversized double entrance doors. The sheer magnitude of the house is a little overwhelming. When we arrive at the front door, Hildy suddenly stops. The flutter of her hand on the doorknob displays her discomfort. And just before she pushes the door open, she looks back over her shoulder to Bill and me. Under the pale glow of the front porch light, I notice that the prominent bruise on her cheek has now darkened in colour. I fight the urge to enclose my arms around her, to tell her everything will be fine.

"Are you certain you want to do this?" There's concern in her voice. "I care for you both. That's why I don't want to hear my parents say such awful things. It will break my heart."

For a moment, Bill and I don't speak.

"It's going to be all right, Hildy," I say, giving her a smile. "We can do this."

"Okay." She turns back to the door. Nodding and taking in a deep breath, she twists the knob in her hand. The door swings open, and we all step into the house.

In the oversized foyer, large gold-framed portraits stretch out across the emerald-coloured walls. The place definitely reflects the ego of someone with money. Over in the middle of the room is a grand wooden staircase with long curving rails welcoming people up to the next level. Turning my head, I catch sight of the full-length mirror fixed to the side wall. I study my reflection. Bill's reflection. We both look so out of place standing here with our scruffy hair and homemade clothes. What on earth was I thinking? I don't have a penny to my name. I could never give her the life she is used to and so rightly deserves. Why would Hildy come to my place every day when she has all of this? Did she pity me? Behind me, Bill's voice breaks the silence bringing me back into the moment.

"Toby, Hildy spoke to you."

"Hmmm," I say, turning around.

"Oh, never mind." Hildy walks to the carved timber doors at the back of the room. She shoves them open and steps through.

Once again, I'm gobsmacked. This room is more elaborate than the last. Red velvet curtains dangle down from every window. Over to the rear of the chamber sits a large mahogany cabinet with polished glass doors displaying a range of expensive bottled whisky. I gaze across the room at the large floral tapered settee that could comfortably seat around ten people. It's certainly different to the old worn out lounge my family uses every day.

At first, I don't notice him sitting there in the shadows. It's not until I catch the cigar smoke curling up to the ceiling that I realise someone's there. From the doorway, I watch him. My first impression is that he could be a banker. I recognise the sort—the upscale suit, the slicked-back hair. He carries the air of a person in authority, someone who doesn't take orders from others.

For the moment, he seems content sitting there, sipping his whisky, watching us. Through the silence, I am now aware of the ticking clock because every ticking pulse beats to the rhythm of my pounding heart.

"Father," Hildy says, moving further into the room, her voice seems upbeat. "I thought I'd find you in here. How was your day?"

He ignores her by eyeing the two strangers standing in the room. His face alters as the disgust rolls out of him in hot waves. His glare runs through me like a sword. A lump the size of a cricket ball forms in the back of my throat.

Time seems to lengthen as he sips his drink. A second later, he places the glass down on the table beside him and then lifts himself out of the armchair. He takes one more puff on his cigar before he puts it down into the silver ashtray. The moment he glances back at us, his whole face changes. A crease on his forehead forms; the muscles at the side of his mouth twitch.

It's enough to send a chill through my entire body.

"Get the hell out of my house!" He barges across the room, yelling at us. "What are you doing here with my daughter?"

"No, father!" Hildy screams from the other side of the room.

Before I know it, he has my arms pinned down to my sides. The weight of him hurls me back against the wall.

"You won't get a penny from her or from me, you hear?" His hand closes in around my throat. His alcoholic breath falls against my skin.

Now I find it impossible to breathe. My lungs burn; my brain swells.

Bill drops his shoulder between the two of us. The momentum rips us apart. Just as I'm about to fall on the ground, Bill collects me in his arms. I suck in great gulps of air to help dissipate the pain surging through my chest.

Hildy's father straightens up. Standing in front of us, eyeing us, he smooths back the loose strands of hair that have fallen out of place. "I said get out."

Bill releases his grip and steps forward. "Look, Cecil is it?" He holds his palms up as if surrendering. "We're not here to cause you any trouble. We came here to explain what happened to Hildy and my brother today."

For a moment, Cecil lets the words hang in the air as if deciphering what Bill has said. "Why? What happened to Hildy?" He pivots, locating her in the back of the room. His mouth falls open. "Dear God, what have they done to you?"

His words make my insides contract.

"No! No, Father. It's nothing like that." She moves forward. "These two boys would never hurt me. They've been nothing but kind and sweet."

"Well, then, you need to tell me what happened to you." His expression shifts to a look of confusion.

There is silence as Hildy's eyes flick over to me. She seems a little lost for words as if unsure where to start. When I don't move, her eyes transfer across to Bill.

He steps forward. "Here, let me explain what—"

"What is all the commotion in here? I can barely think with all this noise!" A voice explodes into the room. In walks a sophisticated-looking woman. I can only assume she is Hildy's mother, Martha, because the resemblance is unnerving. She stops immediately when her eyes fall on the two undesirables standing only inches away from her. Just the mere sight of us makes her whole body stiffen. She lifts her head and peers down her nose with undisguised hatred. "And may I ask what *they* are doing here?"

As I stare at her, I take in her eyes, which are the same shade of green as Hildy's. This beauty standing in front of us could easily pass as Hildy's sister rather than her mother. But the moment her emerald eyes bore deep into my soul, I can no longer see the likeness. I see only ugliness. I now comprehend that mother and daughter are nothing alike.

"Listen," Bill tries to interject before the situation escalates.

"Don't you dare tell me to listen!" Disgust crosses Martha's face as if she had just caught wind of an open sewer. "How dare you insult me by speaking to me?"

"We don't want any trouble."

While Bill tries to reason with Martha, Hildy and I share a concerned look.

"I was trying to tell Cecil here what happened today. That's all."

The room falls silent.

Bill opens his mouth to speak but closes it the moment Martha turns her back on him. Her eyes locate Hildy standing at the back of the room.

"You were with these two worthless things?" Her voice pierces through the room, prompting a short, awkward silence.

"No!" Hildy shakes her head. "Don't you dare be so horrible to them, Mother!"

"I've told you not to have anything to do with people like this, especially the likes of these two." The ferocity in her voice is so harsh, so cold, it jolts right through me. "Do you want to humiliate me in front of society? What if they find out what you've been doing? Oh, you stupid girl. It's people like this—"

"Like what mother?" Hildy cuts in sharply. "Go on. I dare you to say it."

I send another glance to Bill. He doesn't seem to notice. He's too preoccupied with the conversation at hand. For the life of me, I can't understand this woman. Why is she worried about what society thinks? What about Hildy's battered face and what she has been through?

"Just look at them, you silly girl." Martha turns and peers down her nose at us. I swallow nervously under her piercing stare. "Have a good look at them and tell me you don't see the worthless garbage for what they are. They are not your friends, you simple girl. People like this never are."

I peer beyond Martha to see Hildy's face tightening. As tears form in her eyes, I can almost feel the weight of her thoughts.

"That's not true, Mother." Emotion surges into her voice. "They would never manipulate me like that. You don't know them the way I know them. You don't know anything about them. They've been nothing but kind." She sniffs and wipes her face. "You shouldn't judge people because of what everyone else says."

"Oh, you think you know everything about them, do you? You think they're kind. You know nothing, child. People like that—" She turns her head and flicks her wrist in our direction. "They're not your friends. They're only kind to you because they want our money. Can't you see that?"

Hildy shakes her head. The tears shimmer down across her cheeks. "No! No! There is no way they would be like that."

I stride forward, frantically needing to go over there, to wrap my arms around her, to transfer her back to my way of life and away from all of this. I get it now. I understand why she came to us, why she never wants to leave when it's time to go.

But before I advance any further, Bill clutches my arm and keeps me anchored.

"Let me go."

"No, you will only make it worse for her."

"We have to do something, Bill."

He nods, drops my arm, and turns his attention back to the discussion in the middle of the room. "Um ... just to clear things up, we don't want your money." He speaks loud enough to interrupt the conversation on the other side of the room.

Martha halts and swings her pinched-off face toward him.

"And I feel I should also point out, regardless of what you think, that my brother and I aren't garbage." He tilts his head, mocking Martha with a wise-cracking smile. "I'm sure the word *garbage* means something else. But I thought you would have known that, considering you're the more superior one in the room, apparently."

I shut my eyes for a moment, silently cursing myself for listening to him. I should have just gone over there myself instead of letting him toy with Martha for his own satisfaction. How is that going to make it better for Hildy?

"Bill." Hildy steps forward, wiping her eyes with the back of her hands. "It's okay. I can do this."

He nods. A smile plays over his lips.

"Mother, see those two boys over there? The ones you claim are garbage? You should know that it is because of them that I know what it feels like to have someone care about me—for just being myself and not for our money. You're too ignorant to realise people care about us only because of the money. You're the stupid one for not seeing that."

Martha's mouth falls open.

"And, yes, they may be a little different to what you're used to, but they make me feel happy and free. Free of all restraints. You look down your nose at them because you see only their external side. You don't see what I see, and you never will. Every day I witness their kindness and their love and appreciation for everything they have in this world. Oh, Mother, if only you could see this, then you might think differently about your life. Instead, you believe what everyone tells you. All you worry about is money and what society thinks. You can't even see what's right under your nose. You have two daughters who have wanted your approval and love for all these years. Now I don't care about your approval anymore. I don't care what you think. If I had to decide between you and those two boys,

I would choose them in a heartbeat any day. It's as simple as that."

Hildy's words hit Martha like a sledgehammer, and I watch her face stiffen. "You say that now, but wait six months down the track when you come to live their pathetic life. You'll soon see they rely on us to throw a penny here and there. They wouldn't survive without us." She pauses for a moment as a catlike smile spreads across her lips. "I'm sure the authorities would love to hear how those two boys broke into this house to steal our things, and in the process, they hurt you and your sister."

Thoughts rush into my mind. I swallow as my pulse races.

Hildy stands stunned, staring at her mother with an open mouth. "B-but they did nothing, and you know that. Please, please don't do this."

"I can do whatever I like, young lady. I'm the one in charge here. You seem to have forgotten that." She gives Hildy a long, stern glare. "What on earth are you wearing? "

Hildy looks down and smooths her hand over the front of the dress as if wiping away an imaginary crease.

"Go. I can't stand looking at you in that … that hideous thing. You look like that crazy woman. Now get out of my sight. I've had enough of your antics today."

Hildy and I share a quick look. We both know what's coming.

"Don't you talk about my mother like that!" Bill's voice rises dangerously.

"How dare you speak to me like that!"

"Well, don't talk about my mother like that!"

"I'm only telling the truth, and I can't possibly take back the facts, now can I?" She lifts her chin, and her mouth twists into a bitter smile. "I am not known to tell lies." The words hang as she saunters around the room.

"Oh, you want to play a game of truth, do you?" Bill crosses his arms up over his chest and stands his ground. "Well, let's play, shall we? Let me first start by saying it's no wonder Hildy came looking for some motherly love." He grins and keeps his eyes locked on Martha. "She came to us because she ain't getting any love from the cold-hearted bitch of a mother she has waiting at home."

Martha looks stunned by Bill's accusation. Her face goes stark white, and her mouth hangs open. Her body is more rigid than it was before. "Get out, you worthless piece of crap!" She is no longer the sophisticated woman who entered the room only minutes ago. Her scowl darts to Cecil as if silently instructing him to take control.

In the next second or two, Cecil lets out a roar and pushes his hands around Bill's throat, thrusting him back into the wall.

Bill claws wildly at the hands around his throat. His eyes bulge. Thick veins protrude over his face.

As all this happens, I stand there watching as if it is all playing out in a dream. It isn't until I hear Hildy's scream that I come to. I throw all my body weight behind my shoulder, hitting them both, knocking them sideways against the wall. Pain projects through my body. It's like colliding with a freight train. With the last bit of effort I can muster, I straighten up and hobble off to one side. All I can do now is see how it unfolds.

Bill shies sideways, dodging Cecil's grasp. Instantly enraged, Cecil drives his body behind his punch. It smashes Bill in the jaw, jolting his head back. The blood pools at the side of his mouth. Bill wipes it quickly with the heel of his hand.

Cecil moves in for the attack. Somehow he grabs Bill by the arm and forcefully twists it high up behind Bill's back. They both fall clumsily to the floor. For a few long seconds, Bill's face is forced down against the floor. Cecil is now in control.

He presses his body down, pinning Bill to the floor. He reaches out, snatches a fistful of hair, and yanks Bill's head back to hiss something into his ear.

Whatever he says causes Bill to react. Bill jerks his head back, striking Cecil hard in the face. Bright red blood oozes down from the man's nostrils. Breathing hard, Bill's the first one to get to his feet. He waits for Cecil, who seems stunned and slow to curl his legs underneath him. When he eventually stands and straightens up, Bill draws back his fist and ploughs it into Cecil's stomach, making him stumble backward. He crashes into furniture, scattering an expensive-looking vase full of flowers. His legs fold beneath him as he slumps to the floor. Bill stands over Cecil, watching his will to fight slowly dissolve.

When Cecil is no longer a threat, Bill turns and discovers I'm leaning against the wall, arm crossed up over my chest, nursing my ribs.

"Are you okay?" He races to my side and stands me upright.

"Yeah."

The tension in the chamber has somewhat eased a little now that Bill has the upper hand. He takes a few steps back and searches for Hildy.

Tears are rolling down her cheeks, and her lower lip is quivering.

Bill rushes over to her side. "Are you all right?" He reaches up and wipes the tears from her face with his fingers.

"I told you." She sniffs as she looks up into his face. "I told you it was impossible."

"I'm sorry, Hild." He curls his fingers around her hand. "I didn't understand."

Martha's voice screeches through the room. "I think it's time you left."

"We will," Bill concedes, keeping his eyes focused on Hildy. "But first, I made a promise."

"I'll be okay, Bill." Hildy views her mother for a quick second before looking back to Bill. "It might be easier, though, if you were to leave. I'll be fine."

He lingers there for a long while staring at her face. "I'm sorry. We should have listened." He pulls her in close for a quick embrace and then turns and retreats to my side. Supporting my elbow, he escorts me over to the door.

In one last attempt to see her, I peek back over my shoulder. The final image I have of Hildy is her wet glistening face as she watches us move to the door.

10

We've only just got back to the house, and already Bill's asking a million questions. I don't want to answer any of them. All I want is to be left alone.

I shuffle down the hallway; Bill races behind.

"Do you think what I said will get Hildy into trouble?" He stares at me. "Well?"

I ignore him and step into my room, and even though he is still talking, I shut the door in his face. Empty of everything, I lean back against the door. The walls that were strong for Hildy come crashing down. My bottom lip trembles. The tears overflow and course down the sides of my face, pooling at the base of my chin. It's only a matter of seconds before my legs buckle underneath me and my body slides down the length of the door. I hunch my shoulders as harsh sobs rack through my body.

Torturous howls fall from my mouth one after the other, like continual waves washing over the shore, broken only by small lapses that allow enough time for me to catch my breath before I break down again.

The hours pass. I stay there, unmoving, unblinking. Alone in the smothering darkness, the torment continues.

The world is silent as the new morning rays of light soak across the land. I get up and pull the door open. The squeaky hinges scream out into the silence. I stare down the empty hall. Aside from my own breathing, there are no other sounds. No one is up yet. With caution, I step out into the hallway. The noisy boards creak in under my feet.

I'm almost at the end of the hall when I hear Bill whisper from behind. It startles me, making my heart thump against my sternum.

"Where are you going?"

I twist around and discover him leaning against his bedroom door, arms folded up over his chest.

"It doesn't matter." I stare at him for a few long seconds, momentarily stunned by his unexpected appearance. "Just go back to bed." I turn away and continue moving further down the hall.

"No. I can't sleep. I wouldn't go, brother." He races around me and gives an irritated shake of his head.

"How did ..." I look surprised. Then I straighten up. "Get out of my way." I stare hard at him.

No reaction.

I breathe out my nose in frustration. "Get out of my way, Bill. I need to see her right now."

"You can't go there."

"You can't stop me."

"If I have to, I will."

"Don't think just because you're older that I can't kick your arse, because I will."

Bill sets his shoulders back and takes a deep breath. "Have a look at yourself. You look like crap. You're still dressed in yesterday's bloodied clothes. You haven't even showered."

A sheen of tears glaze over my eyes as I search his face. "Yeah, so? What's your point?"

"My point is you can't go. What if her parents see you?"

"I don't care about her damn parents. I need to see *her*." As I talk, I circle around him. "And since when do you care about following rules?"

"I don't." He jerks my arm back, trying to stop me.

I flinch in pain and let out a groan. "Just mind your own business, Bill."

"Sorry." Bill eases his way in front of me. "It doesn't matter what I say. You're still going, aren't you?"

"Yep."

A moment passes. Still, Bill doesn't move. He stands there watching me, trying to read me. Then a flicker of understanding passes across his face. "Wait."

"Why? So you can talk me out of going there?"

"No, because I'm coming with you. But first, promise me you won't do anything stupid."

"You ought to talk," I scoff. "I'm not the one who called Hildy's mother a cold-hearted bitch."

He looks down at the floor in front. "Yeah, I've been worried about that all night. I hope they don't punish her for what I said."

"I can't think about that now. I need to see her." I push past him.

Bill beats me out the front door and stops at the top of the steps. "Are you certain you want to do this?" He runs a hand back through his hair as he keeps his eyes steady on the landscape in front.

"Remember, I didn't ask you to come," I say firmly. "You can always stay home." His question doesn't surprise me. It's the same question I'd asked myself earlier in the room and have pondered over ever since. But I'm not thinking straight. I have to see her. I have to make sure she's okay. Deep down, I need to know if she blames me.

Bill waits until I've moved down the steps before joining me along the drive. At first, we walk in total silence. It isn't until we're halfway there that Bill starts to bombard me with questions.

"Did Hildy mention anything to you about her parents?"

"Yeah, she did. But I didn't realise it was that bad."

"Can you imagine living like that? To have all of that money and treat your kid like crap because of it?"

The muscles in my jaw contract as I think of the way we left her there last night. The image of her standing there alone, upset, left behind to deal with the punishment her parents would dish out for the simple fact that she knew me. I take a deep breath and push my body to move quicker. I have to see her.

"It looks like her parents couldn't care less about her." Bill shoves his hands into his pockets. "Maybe that's why she came to our house every day. She was seeking a place where she belonged."

"You only just worked that one out?"

He shakes his head. "Nah. I figured that out ages ago."

We turn into Hildy's street. I cast a nervous glance up to the large stone pillars a hundred yards in front as if in some way expecting to see her standing there, waiting for me. That's when I spot the two trucks travelling up the long drive, each loaded up with wooden crates, large tables, and chairs. The first truck carries the floral settee I remember seeing last night. My heart quickens. My nerves tighten.

"Bill," I say.

He stops walking and looks in the direction of my pointed finger. When the image registers in his mind, he gives me a sharp look. Then he's off, feet pounding hard on the road as he bolts towards the driveway. It's as if his life depends on it.

I quicken my pace and watch as the first truck exits the gate. It turns right and drives off down the road. The need to know what the hell is going on sits like a fever under my skin. My eyes automatically shift to the next truck when it exits the gate and then stops in front of the stone pillars. The driver emerges out of the vehicle and rushes over to the large iron gates.

Bill races forward, yelling and waving his hand above his head. The driver chooses to ignore him and continues closing the massive gates. A moment later, he slides in behind the wheel of the truck.

As Bill approaches, the driver turns the vehicle and follows the other truck. Bill stops, catching his breath. Resting his hands on the top of his head, he turns to face me. The air stalls in my lungs as I take in the scene.

Cradling my ribs, I trot forward, gritting my teeth all the way to help cope with the pain.

"She's gone!" Bill yells.

Even as his words register in my mind, I don't want to believe it. I look across to the gates, closed tightly together and bound with a double twisted chain secured with a large, sturdy lock.

"Did you hear me?"

Dumbfounded, I look back to him.

"She's gone, brother." He lifts his shoulders and lets them fall. "She's up and left."

His words pack a powerful punch. The tears rise up in a sneak attack. "No. No. She wouldn't do that. She wouldn't leave without telling me." I press my hand over my mouth, fighting for composure. But the stark truth is there right in front of me.

"They did this because of what I said last night." Bill paces in front of the gate. "Why do I always open my mouth and ruin everything? What's wrong with me?"

Feeling sick and dizzy, I turn away, but not before Bill catches the hurt look on my face. I inch my way back down the road, well aware of the flooding emotions threatening to consume every part of me. My heart is heavy in my chest. It's breaking. And as I walk home, the same loop of thoughts plays through my mind. I question everything. Why did she leave? Why wouldn't she tell me? Did she blame me for all that had happened? At once, the brutal reality of being betrayed, of being abandoned, hits me. All our aspirations of a life together are nothing but forgotten dreams. I feel numb. My legs feel as if they've turned to water, and for the life of me, I can't understand why they haven't collapsed.

The further I walk, the more the pain converts to anger. It pushes up question after question, like tiny pouts of puke, one after the other. I go over it in my head. My stomach turns. A wave of cold washes over me as I come to the same conclusion every time. None of this would have happened if Bill had never left the river.

As I reach the front of the house, my anger is blazing. I stop at the bottom step and twist around sharply to glare at him. "Why did you leave the swimming hole yesterday?"

My voice hits him like a prod, jolting him back from distant thoughts. He looks up at me. "What are you talking about?"

I stand in front of him, fierce and angry. I speak through clenched teeth. "I asked you why you left the swimming hole yesterday. If you hadn't left, then none of this would have happened."

His expression is full of shock, as if my harsh words have slapped him in the face. "What? So, now you're blaming me for what happened to you and Hildy at the river?" He moves forward, pushing his face into mine. "I don't think so. You've said some idiotic things over the years, Toby, but this has to be the dumbest." He gives a glare that suggests there is no point in continuing with the conversation. Shaking his head, he steps aside to move up the steps. I shift to the left, blocking his way.

His eyes lift. The lines in his face are severe. "Sure, it's my fault. Is that what you want to hear? Think about it, brother. Do you know what you're implying?"

I stand my ground and hold his gaze. "Yes, if you hadn't marched off in one of your tantrums. Then just maybe—" I shrug.

"Go on. Say it." He clenches his teeth and gives me a look that could quickly freeze water at thirty feet. "I dare you."

"None of this would have happened. And Hildy wouldn't be gone."

He reaches up and twists the collar of my shirt in around my neck. The momentum pushes me back. "If you want to blame someone, blame the dickhead that hurt her. It's his fault, not mine." He is so angry that tiny flecks of spit come out of his mouth and land over my face. "This one time, I will let it go because you're not thinking straight. But if you ever blame me again for what happened to Hildy at the river, I will kick your arse. Do you understand?" He releases his grip, sidesteps around me, and trudges up the steps.

"Yeah, I'd like to see you try to kick my arse." I turn abruptly, yelling at him as he crosses the verandah. "So what's stopping you now?" I hold balled fist out to him, ready to fight. "Come on, then. I'm ready whenever you are."

"Just go inside, brother." Bill yanks open the screen door. It slams shut as he enters the house.

I don't move. I remain there watching the door long after Bill has gone. I just stand there, alone in all the gloom. Time passes; I'm not sure how much. And then I am walking down the hall, trying to comprehend my loss. I open my bedroom door. The room becomes blurred as I fight to gain control. I choke myself off, not wanting to believe Hildy could do that to me. I wipe the flowing tears from my face. Feeling weak, I settle down onto the bed, pulling the covers in around my neck. I close my eyes believing that all hope is lost. The sorrow washes over me like cold, acid rain. Nausea churns in my stomach. Tears accumulate as my mind slowly shuts down. As I lie there, all hope drains from my soul. I don't want to think anymore. There is nothing left to feel, nothing left to say. Everything I've ever wanted is now lost to me. My heart is broken. My soul is shattered. No amount of glue can ever bond them back together. I stay there for the next four days.

Twenty-One

11

As the years have progressed, our mother's health had diminished significantly. She can no longer remember the names of her sons. She's trapped in her own silent world and has been for the past six months. In her mind, her world has altered back to a time in her youth—a time before children, a time before our father.

Because of that, Bill and I eat our breakfast in silence as we do not want to upset her. Every now and then, we see tiny snippets of the mother we thought we'd lost. In those moments, my mother calls Bill by our father's name. It's only happened three times over the last four months, but in those sweet moments, Bill gets to communicate with her.

The first time it happened, Bill tried to include me in the conversation, but the minute I spoke, my mother withdrew and retreated to her room. So the next time it happened, I sat there quietly, savouring the moment. It was so wonderful to see her that way again. I have to admit it hasn't been easy watching her wilt away into a shell of the person she once was. It saddens me to think she will never know the men we have become, the men she raised.

Onto other matters now. I am pleased to report I am two inches taller than Bill, much to his disappointment.

Neither one of us has heard from Sam for a while now. He secured a job at the local bakery where he met a girl and fell madly in love. Early on, he would drop by every second or third day, always bringing with him a fresh loaf of bread. But as time took over and life got in the way, his visits became more limited. Bill misses him. It's obvious, although he would never acknowledge that. And it is for that reason that Bill and I have grown closer. We've ended our "one up" moments. I'm not sure if it's because we have matured or because of the simple fact that we now understand we have no one else in this world except each other.

As for Hildy, there's nothing new to report. Bill continued to check those gates for another two weeks. And still today they remain closed.

Even though Hildy's not around, I still see her everywhere. If I'm walking into town or watching the sky split, then tiny fragments of our time spent together creep back into my mind. Over time, my body healed, but my soul will be forever broken. Every day it's torture not having her near. There's an ache that comes to me in those quiet moments, a sense of sadness that strangles my veins. I desperately want to keep her close, remember what it felt like to hold her, to talk to her, and to laugh the way we used to.

I haven't ventured down to the river or through the wildflowers. Honestly, I don't think my head or my heart could take it.

Earlier on, just after she left, at night, when I was alone in my room, I'd give in and surrender to the pain. It was easier that way. I'd fill my mind with her image, close my eyes, and allow the tears to spill. I had to stop myself from doing that because of the terrible dreams. Every time it's always the same. I'm standing with Hildy in the valley of the wildflowers. She looks over and smiles. We're happy. We're the way we used to be—those beautiful innocent kids. But the moment I reach out and slip my hand into hers, everything changes. The dazzling sun melts into dark, looming clouds, and unexpectedly the air chills around us. Tree branches twist and turn into ghostlike shapes. The blossoming flowers wilt and crumple around our feet. Then a streak of lightning flashes across the sky, and the stranger is there, glaring at us with his wolflike eyes. Panic consumes every cell in my body. With desperation, I yank on Hildy's hand to pull her away, but for some reason, I can't make her move. In a panicked state, she screams out my name. I wake, saturated, sucking large gulps of air back into my lungs. I'm twenty-one years of age, and still I feel like a child again running away from the boogie man.

So, I've had to come up with creative ways to avoid those frightful dreams. Over time, I've discovered that, if I work hard at Picker's farm, especially on those sweltering days out in the scorching sun, then I have control because my body's too exhausted to dream. Tonight I will not experience any such horror because I've been out fixing fences in the hot sun.

As Bill and I wrap up our shifts at the end of a long day, we make our way home.

As usual, Bill's the first one through the door, still racing in, tossing his wide-brimmed hat off to one side, plopping down onto the old lounge, dirty boots and all.

"If you're getting a drink, then get me one too," he yells at my passing back.

"No. Get it yourself." Walking down the hall, I wipe the sweat and dust from my face. Less than three feet away from the door, I am startled to see my mother's body lying face down on the kitchen floor. I let go of the tin lunch box in my hand. It bounces loudly across the floorboards.

"Bill, get in here now!" I sprint across the room and drop to my knees. "Mum! Oh, God, please be okay! Mum!" I reach out, grab her by the shoulders, and roll her onto her back. "Answer me, Mum! Please say something." The second my eyes take in her ghastly pale skin and her open blue eyes, my hands recoil.

"What do you want now?" Bill shouts down the hall. The moment he arrives in the open doorway, his whole body stiffens. "Jeeze, what the hell happened?" He hurtles himself through the room and collapses on his knees beside me. "Mum, can you hear me?" He leans over and holds two fingers in under her nose, feeling for her breath.

My mother's eyes, which always sparkled with so much light, stare vacantly up at the ceiling. Her mouth, which laughed thousands of times, is now cold and motionless. Seeing her this way makes me feel as if I have died myself.

"She's gone, Bill," I say, scooting backward across the floor.

He doesn't hear me.

"Come on, Mum," he mumbles, propping the back of his hand up against her forehead.

"Bill, will you listen?" My voice is emotional. "We're too late. She's passed."

"No! No." His whole face drops as he stares up at me through misty eyes.

The entire world suddenly turns cold.

A single tear drips down over my cheek, and just like that, the floodgates are forced open. I lift myself up onto my feet, and then it hits me like a sledgehammer to the gut—death has taken her away from us. A huge knot twists and tightens in my stomach. I feel as if every breath is being stolen away from me. I can't handle it. I don't want to see her like this. I don't want to listen to the sound of Bill's sobbing. It's all too much. I bolt from the kitchen.

As soon as I make it out the front door, vomit explodes from my mouth. I vomit over and over again until there is nothing left to bring up. The pressure that is strangling my heart forces me down onto my knees. I bury my head in my hands, all the while wondering how I will ever exist in a world from which my mother is absent. The thought forces me to howl like a tiny child.

I don't know how long I stay out there like that. It's all a blur. All I remember is Bill coming out onto the front porch, picking me up off the floor, and planting me in one of the chairs. He doesn't utter a single word. He just walks back into the house. I sit there in my trance-like state staring numbly out over the land. Time seems to slow as the veil of sadness and death floats freely over the house. It is not until I see a figure zipping by that I come back into the moment.

"Where are you going?" I sit forward in the chair.

Bill pauses on the bottom step and keeps his back facing me. "I'm going in to see the priest."

"Wait. I'm coming with you." I stand.

"No, you're not." He turns around. I notice his red-rimmed eyes. "You don't have to come. I can do this alone, Toby."

"I know you can, Bill. Please let me come into town with you." I swipe the wetness away from my face with the back of my hand. "We can do this together. I can help you." The truth is that a part of me needs to get away from the house. I can't stay here alone with my mother's lifeless body only in the next room.

I climb down the steps. Bill's eyes stay focused on me. His expression carries nothing but misery. "Okay. But only if you want to." His words are soft; they expose his vulnerability.

I nod.

"Thank you, brother. I'm not sure I can do this alone." He blows out a breath. Turning around, he leads the way down the drive.

We walk in silence down the main street, turn right at the intersection, and cross over the road to the only church in town. As we stand there, the memories seep in. I am taken back to that ten-year-old boy sitting between my mother and my brother, all of us dressed in our best Sunday clothes. That was the first time I ever heard the rumours. I couldn't understand why people were watching us as we walked down the aisle to sit in our regular seats. Not one person spoke, even when my mother greeted them in her usual cheery manner. They only whispered behind her back.

The moment Father McGuire stopped at the end of our pew, the whole place fell silent. In front of the whole congregation, he asked us to leave. He told us the community felt uneasy now that the devil had possessed my mother's mind. At such a young age, I didn't know what to make of his words because we had been taught to fear the devil. It was Bill who put me at ease when he defended our mother, and in doing so, he also created a process he would continue to repeat over the years. I cannot begin to imagine the cruel humiliation my mother must have felt that day as she walked us back down the aisle, knowing everyone thought we didn't belong.

The silence is unsettling as we stand there. Somewhere in the street, I hear a car door slam, and within seconds, I hear the motor start up and the vehicle drive away. I turn my head sideways to find Bill frozen on the spot, shoulders hunched, eyes set forward on the church. He sucks in a breath and then, as if galvanised back into life, he moves up the staircase. I follow him like a shadow the entire time.

Bill pushes open the sturdy wooden double doors. We step through. I flinch as I remember the sound they made when they shut behind us so long ago. The dread of rejection fills me once again. We walk along the passageway. My eyes pick up the afternoon light streaming in through the stained-glass windows. The glorious beams of sunlight spear around the room. I have forgotten how beautiful it is in here. The fragrance of incense awakes an old memory, a happier time when Bill and I clung to our mother's skirt as she escorted both of us over to our seats. I turn my head. In my mind, I visualise my mother sitting there in the pew dressed in her Sunday dress.

A door at the rear of the chapel abruptly swings open. In walks the priest. I feel my heart give a thud. He pauses and glares at us from behind thin-rimmed glasses, and his mouth puckers as if tasting something sour. "What are you two boys doing in here?"

At the sound of his voice, Bill swallows, straightens, and moves down the aisle. "Well ..." He clears his throat. "We came here because our mother died today."

Father McGuire's eyes move from Bill and land on me. I rub the sudden pain I feel in my stomach.

"I am sorry for your loss, but it was probably for the best."

"How can you say that?" Bill shuffles forward, agitated.

I reach out and tap Bill's arm for him to back down.

Father McGuire studies us for a moment. The time and silence stretch.

I step around Bill and take control of the conversation. "Look, Father, we came here to organise a burial for our mother, that's all. There will be only Bill and me. Oh, and Mr. Picker. He'll want to attend. Anytime is fine with us." I inhale a shaky breath and await a response.

He stares at me stone-faced.

"Father, I—"

"No need. I heard what you said." His mouth coils in a strange bitter smile as he turns away and heads for the table over on the side wall. "That is not a good idea."

I arch my eyebrows. "I don't understand what you mean."

He spins around with such fury that his next words spit from his hard mouth. "It's preposterous! That's what I'm saying. What would the community think if I let you bury her here?" He snatches a silver goblet from the table and stands before us as if challenging either one of us to speak.

My heart beats a little faster. "Now hang on a minute." I try to keep my voice steady, but it's rising slightly. "Where are we supposed to bury her?"

"That's not my problem."

I watch him pace across the room. This can't be happening. Even in death, she is still an outcast. I shake my head and look away from him to the coloured-glass windows. My breath comes out fast and hard.

Bill brushes past me. "What do you mean you won't bury her here? Everyone gets buried here. Even old Harry, the town thief, is buried out there."

Dizziness hits me. It tilts me off to one side so that I have to take a seat.

The priest places the chalice down on the altar. Interlocking his fingers, he rests his hands over his large belly. "There will be no funeral here. You need to make other arrangements."

Bill moves forward down the aisle until he stands right in front of the priest, just close enough to invade his personal space. "I don't care what you think about her, or even us for that matter. My mother needs a burial."

"And how do you think the community will react when they find out I let you bury her here?"

My brain swims. The community. The big question is what do we do with our mother?

"That's all I will say on this matter. Now off you go. I have work to finish." He dismisses us by turning his back.

Bill cuts me a look. There's a sheen of tears glazing his eyes. Shoving his hands into his pockets, he stares out across the empty church before moving back toward the door. I stand and follow him along the aisle.

Halfway to the door, Bill abruptly stops. Filled with anger, he turns to the priest. He makes a growling sound and storms back down the aisle. "Stuff the community and stuff you!" His voice is so cold that a shiver runs right through me.

Father McGuire spins around, his face frozen with shock as Bill rages on.

"All of you are a bunch of hypocrites! You all assume the devil had a hold of my mother's mind. But it was you who let the devil through those doors the day you told us to leave. You don't live by God's teachings. You only abide by the rules of those who can stuff money into your pockets. The power of money is your god!"

Father McGuire now looks as if someone has punched him in the larynx.

"God isn't contained in these walls," continues Bill. "Don't you dare tell me my mother isn't worthy of this church! She died." He swallows, and I hear his voice soften. "She was the one who taught us right from wrong, something you could never teach. She was the one who taught us to be kind and to love one another no matter what others thought. It was *her*. Not *you*. You only encourage people to hate or even to despise. You encourage them to mistreat people until they become outcasts in the community. That's what you did. You and your so-called churchgoers. So you can stick your teachings right up your arse. She doesn't need you or your puppet masters judging her in her final resting place." He turns. "Come on, brother. We don't have to put up with this shit."

Father McGuire looks hard at me from the front of the altar as Bill brushes back past me.

"He's right you know," I add. "You did all of that. On the day of your passing, let's hope it's God who collects your soul and not the devil." I turn my back on him and follow Bill down the walkway.

12

Great sadness and anger weigh us down as we arrive back at the house. I stagger up onto the verandah to take a seat. I cannot make myself go inside. Bill sits doubled over on the staircase, eyes focused down on the step beneath him.

As the seconds tick, I look at him out the corner of my eye. He is shaking and extremely pale in a way that makes him look sick.

The question as to what to do with my mother curves and swoops in my mind. "Bill, what are we going to do?"

He doesn't answer. Time passes. I'm not sure how much, but I know the sun is starting to dip towards the horizon.

Not saying a word, Bill hoists himself up from the step and starts off toward the old shed.

"Where are you going?" I yell, sitting forward in the chair.

"Nowhere."

A moment later, I catch him advancing across the front yard. There's a shovel resting high on his shoulder.

"Bill, what are you doing?"

"Don't worry about it. I'll take care of it."

I bolt down the stairs. "Bill, tell me what you are doing!"

"What does it look like?"

The realisation comes and slaps me in the face. My entire body shudders as my brain tries to fathom why he's even considering the idea. I shake my head. "No! No, Bill. It's not right. You can't do that."

He steps around me and continues to walk. "What else am I supposed to do?"

"Bill."

He stops but keeps his back facing me. "What?"

I slowly circle around him. "You can't be serious. We don't do it this way, and you know it."

He looks up at me through misty eyes. "If you've got a better idea, then tell me." His voice shakes. "Please tell me, brother. I beg of you." His lips tremble; deep agony oozes from his eyes.

As I search for an answer, I swallow hard. "Picker!" I burst out the first thing that comes to mind.

"What?" His blue eyes narrow.

"We'll get Picker to see the priest." Words spurt out; I'm surprised my brain can catch up. "He goes to church every week. Maybe he can get Father McGuire to bury Mum on the quiet. No one will have to know about it. She could have an unmarked grave. It could work. We need to see Pick—" I watch him walk away.

When he reaches the old gum tree, he lowers the shovel to the ground and uses his boot to drive the blade into the earth.

With a sense of desperation, I try to sprint down the driveway, but it's awkward and slow. My mind and body don't seem to want to work together.

I bolt out through the front gate and charge into Picker's farm. I shriek as I slide on loose gravel. The urgency burns through my veins. As I run, I search for him everywhere. I check the fields, the hay shed, the wheat storage tower. Finally, I locate him in the stables.

"Mr. Picker! Mr. Picker!" My breath comes out too fast, too hard. I can't speak. The words jam in my throat.

"What is it, Toby?" He stops brushing a horse and looks up.

"You have to come." I stoop over. Resting my hands on my knees, I suck in another breath. "Bill's gone mad."

"Why? What is it? What's happened?" He sets the brush down on top of the cupboard.

"It's our mother." Another gulp of air. "When we got home today, we found her. She's dead."

"Oh, Toby, what can I do?"

"We've been in to see Father McGuire, but he won't do it. He won't let us bury her in the cemetery." Sudden tears fill my eyes.

"Well, that's not right." He peers down to his wristwatch, checking the time. "You go back to Bill. I'll see Father McGuire and find out what's going on." He strides over to the truck. I walk beside him, his hand resting on my shoulder. "It will be okay. We'll sort this out."

He gets in, and I watch him take off down the drive.

By the time I arrive back at the house, Bill's already dug a significant hole, a few feet deep.

He stops digging and swipes his brow with the back of his hand. "Where did you go?"

"Over to Picker's."

"What for?" He shrugs. "There's nothing he can do."

"You don't know that, Bill. He's gone into town to see the priest. Maybe he can persuade him."

He straightens up and looks down into the hole. "It doesn't matter who goes in there. Nothing's gonna change. If there was a different way of doing this, don't you think I would take it?" His voice softens. "Our mother loved this place. She'll be happy here with us."

As he breathes heavily through his mouth, I stare at him for the longest time.

"It's the only way." He shrugs and goes back to shovelling. "You don't have to do any of it. I'm the oldest. It's my responsibility."

"Why don't you wait until we hear from Picker?"

"Because that's only prolonging it. This has to be done tonight."

"But you might be digging for nothing."

"I'll take my chances." He digs out another shovel load of dirt, flinging it over onto the pile. He looks up at me. "You can stay and talk about it, but I gotta get this hole dug."

The thought of burying my mother makes me sick to my stomach. Deep down, though, I know he is right. If Picker can't reverse Father McGuire's decision, then there is no alternative; we will have to bury her here.

"I'll get another shovel, and I'll help."

"I thought you were waiting for Picker." He glances up.

My eyes and throat wash with tears. "She is my mother too, Bill. I can't leave you to do it all by yourself."

He nods. Pushing the shovel into my chest, he steps around me and goes back to the shed.

When he re-emerges carrying another shovel as well as a kerosene lamp, I've already scooped out around ten shovel loads. He places the lantern down, and under the soft light, we dig from either side of the hole.

Two hours later, when the land's settled down for the night, we stop digging. Still there is no word from Picker. Exhausted and out of breath, we throw our shovels off to one side and drop our weary bodies onto the ground.

As I draw air into my lungs, I stare up at the glimmering stars and think about how my life has altered today. Now my mother will exist only in my memory. There will never be a tomorrow with her. I will no longer find her sitting in the kitchen sewing one of her quilts. I know that one day her voice will be foreign to me. The pain squeezing on my heart will definitely scar it. It's as if a piece of me is no longer here. Clearing my throat, I wipe my grotty fingers under both eyes and then look across to Bill. He's not there. I jolt up onto my elbow, peer out into the night, and try to remember when he left. The screen door bangs. I turn to see, in the moonlight, Bill stepping down off the front verandah.

Suddenly, two headlights swing into the drive. I get up onto my feet and shiver. Bill stops like an animal dazzled by headlights. It's only then that I see what he's carrying. The colour zaps right out of my face when I realise it's my mother's body wrapped in one of her beautiful quilts.

Time seems to go in slow motion. The vehicle parks in front of the house. It takes a few moments before the headlights go out. In the darkness, I hear two doors slam. My eyes take a while to adjust before I'm able to make out that the two shadowy beings are Picker and Sam.

They round the edge of the yard and stop to chat with Bill. I hear Picker's voice, but I can't make out exactly what he is saying. Bill stands there, saying nothing. A few seconds later, his head turns in my direction, followed shortly by Picker's and Sam's. They all remain quiet for the longest time. My mind pulses with assumptions; my chest becomes tighter. The delay is too much to take.

"What?" I yell out. "What did Father McGuire say?"

Bill twists away from them and strides forward, towards the grave. He looms larger and larger with every step.

"What happened, Mr. Picker?"

"We couldn't find him."

"What do you mean?" A chill passes right through me as I glance across the yard to Picker. "I don't understand how you couldn't find him."

"I searched everywhere, Toby—the church, his home." He wanders over; Sam follows. "I grabbed Sam here to help look and save time, but no one could say where he was. I'm sorry."

"He's probably off sipping someone's expensive wine," says Bill.

"Or stuffing his gut with their food," Sam adds.

I lower my eyes. Bill has already arranged our mother's body on the ground near my feet. I retreat a few steps. The image of the bundle that is her dead body fills my whole being. I have to shift my feet to steady myself.

Bill turns his head. Breathing deeply, he studies me for a long, unsettling minute before he drops down into the hole.

My head throbs to the beat of my heart. I am sick to my stomach with the thought that we are doing this.

Picker's voice cuts through the silence. "Bill, are you certain you want to do this?" Picker takes a step forward. "Why don't you wait until tomorrow when I can find the priest and arrange something?"

"It doesn't matter who confronts him. He's never gonna budge. He made that clear to us earlier today." Bill shifts up one end of the hole. "Are you ready, brother?"

I am lost somewhere between reality and disbelief. My head hurts. How can anyone be ready for this?

Picker's voice again. "Why don't you boys let me do this for you? You don't have to do it. I can do it."

"No, I'm fine. I must do this." Bill moves into position. "But you can take Toby's spot if ya want."

I walk backwards away from the grave, allowing Picker enough room to manoeuvre around her body. He squats down and shifts his hand in under my mother's back. With Bill's help, they slide her over to the edge of the pit. Bill shoves his shoulder in and takes the weight of her body.

From above, I watch him position her body down into her final resting place. Nobody other than Bill will ever comprehend this loss. My soul bleeds knowing no one, other than the four people standing here, cared for her. All anyone saw was that horrible disease. In their eyes, it is what defined her. Deep down, I know there was someone else, but I can't bring myself to think of Hildy. I was already in enough pain.

Using all the power in his arms, Bill hauls himself up out of the grave. "Just let me get one more thing before we fill it in." He rushes off across the yard.

My eyes stare at him vaguely as he stops at the overgrown rose bush at the front of the house. When he returns, he carries two red roses in each hand.

Once he's passed them around, he steps up to the edge of the hole, takes a big breath and then speaks. "Mum, I think you're gonna like it out here under this old gum. I remember when you used to stand under it watching Toby and me climb over the long branches. You always seemed to worry that one of us would fall." He gives a slight smile as the memory comes back to mind. "I'm sorry for all the mischief I got into as a kid."

He draws in another deep breath and runs his thumb in under his eye, swiping the lone tear. "Thank you for all you have done for me and for Toby and everything you taught us over the years. We are so lucky that you are our mum. You created such happiness in our world. And I will miss you more than you will ever know. The pledge I made to you all those years ago still stands. I promise I will look after him for you. You have my word. I love you, Mum. I always will." He stands still, then slowly uncurls his fingers, releasing the rose. He falls back into line. "It's your turn now, brother."

I glance up at him, blinking through misty eyes. "Not yet. Someone else can say something. I'm not ready yet."

Picker clears his throat, steps forward, and cups his hands over his belly. "Oh, Hazel, where shall I start? Over the years you've had such a tough time, but through it all, you kept your dignity. You are one classy lady. Even with all your struggles, you still raised your boys right. They're hard working, loyal, and honest. You should be proud of them. I know I am. You rest now, knowing your boys will be okay. I'll see to that." He lets go of the rose and slips back into line.

I wipe the tears from my eyes. When I lift my head, I find Bill's doing the same.

Next, Sam steps forward. "Mrs. M, I never really had a mum, so I kind of considered you to be mine. You fed me whenever I was here. You put up with all my ridiculous jokes with Bill." He grins and gives a soft laugh. "All those days when you marched me back into town with Bill ... I'm sorry you had to do that. Never once did you get angry or raise your voice. You always guided that naughty, spirited side of me. You have taught me those life lessons that I will always carry. So thank you." He chews down on his bottom lip and releases the rose.

Bill reaches out. His hand trembles on my shoulder.

With a lump lodged in the back of my throat, I move up to the edge. Feeling awkward, I'm not sure what to say. My words will never be enough. I pinch my eyes shut, but the tears spill anyway.

"Come on, Toby, say your last goodbye to Mum, and then you can go." Bill's voice surges with emotion.

Scraping together all the strength I have left, I clear my throat and open my eyes. "Mum," I begin. My voice is frail. "You will always live in my heart no matter where I am. You taught me to love this world for what it is, no matter what challenges we may face each day. To look for the beauty in everything, especially when there's only pain." My lips quiver, and tears gather at the base of my chin. "I love you, Mum. I'm gonna miss you. Look for me when the sky splits, for I will wait there to say hello." I close my eyes, reach my hand out, and uncoil my fingers from around the stem.

When Picker's voice cuts in, I open my eyes and move behind him.

"I can finish up here, lads, if you prefer to head inside."

"No." Bill steps between Picker and me. Crouching down, he collects one of the shovels from the ground. "I have to follow this through. I owe it to my mother. But you can help."

"Come on, Toby," says Sam hunching forward, relaxing his arm on my back. "Let's leave them be."

As Sam and I hike back over the yard, the only noise resonating out into the night air is the chilling sound of loose dirt falling over my mother.

Twenty-Two

13

Another year has passed, and the life I once had is now unrecognisable. My job on Picker's farm is my only link to the outside world. Without it, I fear this house would become my tomb. I can't remember the last time I spoke to Bill. Every day, I arrive home from work to find him passed out in the lounge. He's different now, and I can't understand why he has chosen this life.

Since our mother's passing, Bill has lost his sense of light. Every day, he drowns himself in alcohol. He still has a job on Picker's farm, but he rarely shows up. I'm not sure why Picker hasn't fired him yet. Maybe he feels sorry for the way things have worked out for us. Bill has disappeared from my life. I miss him dearly, especially his laughter.

And, it's because of that isolation I find I'm stuck doing the same routine day after day. I arrive home, cook a meal for one, and then sit out on the back verandah. The unbearable silence is a constant reminder of all that is lost. There is no way of escaping it. A simple whiff of the wildflowers blowing in the breeze triggers all kinds of memories, from walking down to the river with Bill at an early age, to watching Hildy race through the valley. Every little snippet reminds me of what is gone and how it has been ripped away from me, a piece at a time.

I'd like to say I don't think about Hildy, but that would be a lie. She consumes my mind. Every day I seem to mull over the life we dreamed about—the commitment of love and marriage we made to each other. The promise of children. I even dwell on those dreams I once had of working alongside Bill on our own property, earning our own money. That, too, has evaporated. Nothing of it means anything to me now. Someone should have told that naïve eighteen-year-old boy to stop filling his head with unrealistic dreams.

My thoughts vanish the moment I hear the front door slam. It's the first time in three months that Bill's been home early. I push myself up out of the chair and head inside. As I go down the hall, once again the whiff of alcohol hangs in the air.

Quietly, I approach, sneaking a quick peek around the doorway. There, in the middle of the room, I find Bill slouched on the lounge staring out the darkened window. His oily hair and sweat-stained shirt are long overdue for a wash.

I continue to watch him as he leans forward and seizes one of the three bottles of ale from the table in front of him. He pops the cap. Throwing back his head, he guzzles down the brew. My eyes shift to the bright-red lipstick smeared across the collar of his shirt. A year ago, my brother was happy and so full of life, but this unfamiliar person sitting in front of me doesn't seem to care about anything other than alcohol and sex. Many times throughout the previous months, I've wanted to go in there to tell him to snap out of it because I need him. I need my big brother.

When he lowers the bottle, he catches sight of me standing there. "Brother." He smiles.

I move out into the open doorway, giving him a quick smile.

"Where have ya been?" He says, staring up at me through bloodshot eyes. "Come, have a seat."

He studies me as I cross the room and take a seat in the chair opposite.

"Do you want a drink?" He holds the bottle out.

"No."

"Go on," he slurs. Eyes widening, he pushes the glass bottle further out in front. "At least have a toast for Mum. Go on. Just a tiny sip."

"Okay," I give in. History tells me that, if I don't, then he will only persist. His eyes linger as I take a fresh bottle from the table. "But I'm opening a new bottle because I have no idea where your mouth has been."

"Fair enough." He laughs and shakes his head.

I pop off the top.

He lifts his bottle up to make a toast. "To our beautiful mum. May she be in peace now."

"To our mum," I reply, lifting the bottle. As I take a sip, I am aware of Bill's glassy eyes watching me. The second the brown ale strokes the back of my throat, I choke and cough. Liquid sprays from my mouth and oozes down over my chin.

Bill's laughter explodes around the room. It's a glorious sound I haven't heard for so long. I smile as I wipe my chin.

"Don't you like it?"

"No. It's awful." I set the bottle back on the table and look up. "And I don't think it was that hilarious."

"It was from this side." He laughs again.

There's a long silence, during which I eye at least fifteen bottle tops scattered across the floor. When Bill dumps the last of his beer down his throat, I study him critically, wondering what's so appealing about the new lifestyle he has chosen. My mouth twists. I can't hold back. I have to ask.

"Bill, can I ask you something?"

"Yeah, go for it." His eyes slowly lift.

"Where do you go every night?"

"Over to Picker's." He jerks forward and leaves the empty bottle down on the table. "Why do you ask, little bro?"

"So you're drinking with Picker?"

"I wouldn't say that exactly." He scratches his ear and smirks. "I go there to see his daughter."

"Sylvie." I glare at him. It's a good few seconds before I'm able to speak again. "You're drinking with Sylvie?"

"I don't think you could say it's drinking exactly." A smile plays at the edges of his mouth. "But she's a real treat, if you know what I mean." He grabs the bottle I left open on the table and takes a swig.

"Bill, if Picker ever finds out—"

"He won't."

"But if he does—"

He raises his voice. "He won't."

"Well, just make sure he doesn't."

"Yes, Dad." He glances down and studies the bottle in his hand. "Do you want to hear a funny story? It's about Mum." He hesitates, lifts his face, his eyes narrow slightly. "It won't upset ya too much, will it?"

"No." I say, way too fast, shaking my head.

He grins and shifts forward in the lounge. "If I remember correctly, I think I was about eight at the time, or was I nine?"

"It doesn't matter. Let's just say you were nine."

"Okay, you don't have to carry on. Do you remember Millie Edwards? You know that spoilt girl from school, the one who had the boy's haircut?"

I nod slowly.

"There was this one day when she made fun of me in front of the whole class."

"I know where this is heading." I flop back in the chair.

"No. See? You presume." He holds up his forefinger. "This time it was different. I didn't get angry. I wanted to get even. I wanted to embarrass her in front of the whole class like she had done earlier to me." He sniffs and then scratches his fingers through his overgrown beard. "When she sat down in the chair in front of me, I knew it was my chance. I took her long ponytails and pressed them into the inkwell on my desk."

"Oh, no, Bill, you didn't!" I laugh.

He smiles warmly as the memory plays in his head. "Yep, I did. Of course, Sam was there, sitting next to me, encouraging me to push them in further. And I did. Those things practically drowned in it."

"And she didn't know they were in there?"

"No, she didn't." He flashes a toothy grin. "I did it real slow so she couldn't feel it. But guess what? It backfired on me because the teacher called her up to the front of the classroom." He takes a sip of beer.

Sitting there with him, listening, admiring the way he was telling his story, I'm ready to laugh at any moment. Suddenly it feels like old times.

"When she stood up from the desk, I looked down into the inkwell. It was almost empty. I mean you could see the glass bottom."

I laugh out loud. "So, what happened?"

He runs his tongue across his lower lip to exaggerate the suspense just a little longer. "She strolled up to the front of the room, all high and mighty, swinging those pigtails back and forth in that annoying way she always did. Do you remember?"

I don't, but I nod anyway.

"By the time she reached the teacher, she had the stuff everywhere. It was all over her face, over the top of her head, the top half of her frilly dress. Everything was black. You couldn't even see the floral print in the material."

Laughter erupts from my mouth, and I quickly contain it the moment he holds up a finger.

"But that's not the best part." He clears his throat. "The ink wrecked her hair. She had to get it shaved off. And, for that, she hated me even more. The ink discoloured her face for almost a month. Now I'll tell you what happened after that." He slumps back in the lounge and chuckles. "Because I wrecked her dress, Mum had to clean their house for a whole week to pay the money back. Mum took me with her, and as my punishment, she made me clean out Millie's pony stable every day for a month."

Laughter fills the room.

I shake my head at him. "You always got yourself in trouble."

"Yeah, I did."

His words hang in the air.

"Hey, I've got another funny one if you want to hear it."

"Go on."

The laughter and good times continue through the night. I laugh so much that fat tears roll down my face. My stomach muscles ache. At one point, I almost fall off the chair.

As the night keeps going, hearing all his stories somehow makes me feel as if our mother is still alive, still here in this house with us, for the night anyway.

Twenty-Three

14

Another year passes, and the loneliness continues to torment. It's like a wind howling at my soul. Where did it all go so wrong? Nothing seems to matter anymore. All notion of hope is lost. Why is it that every person I've ever loved has left me? Has all my love been wasted? What do I have to show for any of it? A life full of misery and realising I'm all alone in this world.

Why can't my brain erase the memory of Hildy? Day after day, I sit here craving the life we planned together. How can I stop my heart from bleeding for her? I need to find a way to end all this misery. These walls that once carried such beautiful memories now only fill me with complete sadness. Everything here I despise—anything that triggers a memory. A year of isolation has transformed me into a person I don't recognise, or even like for that matter. It's as if someone else has control of the steering wheel, and for the life of me, I have no idea how to get the power back. I detest the person I have become.

Bill still has Sylvie in his intoxicated state, so how pathetic am I?

I thought it would change the day Picker found them together in the back shed, but it didn't. I think a part of me wanted him to experience the same pain I feel so I wouldn't have to go through it all alone. But nothing changed. He didn't care about losing his job. He hadn't been turning up anyway. That night he still went over to Sylvie's and has been doing so ever since.

Now I avoid sitting out on the back verandah. It's easier for me to remain in the shadows of the kitchen. Tonight, as I sit here in the unbearable silence, my thoughts still are haunted. At times it feels as if I'm unable to breathe.

I push up from the chair and move down the hall. Frozen moments of time watch me through dusty panes. I pause when I see my younger self, his tiny eyes fixed on mine. He looks so happy sitting there with Bill, dressed in his best Sunday clothes. If only I could go back in time and change all the events of his life that led up until this moment. I want to protect him, wrap my arms around him, so he never feels this hollow in the deepest part of his soul.

My eyes shift to the next photo. It's my younger mother and father. They seem so happy. I swallow painfully over the sudden lump in my throat as I study my beautiful mother. Her smile is bright and cheerful as she sits there next to my father. My eyes drift to his image. I take in his features. I am well aware that Bill and I possess his exact smile. From out of nowhere, a wave of anger twists inside me. It snakes its way up to the surface.

"Liar!" I yell out to his fake, smug face. "Your smile is nothing but a lie. I hate you for what you did. I hate you for leaving us."

"Brother, is that you?" Bill's voice floats down through the hall.

Eyes fixed on my father's face, I take a breath before stepping back away from the photograph and continue down the hall.

When I find Bill, he's hunched in the lounge, trying to remove his muddy boots. After the fourth attempt and the fact that my patience is wearing thin, I stomp across the room. When I reach him, I purposely move forward to place myself in his space.

He looks up.

The years of drinking have changed him. His once sun-kissed skin now bears an unhealthy grey tinge. His sunken eyes and disturbingly thin cheekbones are the most prominent features of his face. The brother I once had is long gone, and sitting here in his place is a morbid, drunken fool.

"Brother," he says. "It's been a long time."

"You know where to find me." I shove his shoulder with my hand, forcing him back into the lounge. "Just give me your foot before you hurt yourself." He lifts up his leg. With a bit of force and a lot of anger, I remove the boot and set it off to one side.

"Don't be cranky with me," he says. "I haven't seen you in a while. Why don't we have a drink and catch up?"

I reach down and reef up the other leg. "No, I don't think so." This time when I pull off the boot, I let go of his foot. It collapses to the floor, his heel making a loud thud, but he's too drunk to notice.

137

Straightening up, I peer down my nose at him. Our eyes hold briefly for the moment.

"What's wrong with you?" His slurred words hang in the air. He leans forward and snatches a bottle from the table. "What —are you too good to speak to me now?"

"No."

"Then, don't look at me like that." He looks up.

"Like what?"

"Like, you're judging me." His eyes hold mine as he drinks from the bottle.

"Well, I guess if that's what you think, then it has to be true."

"You don't have to be an arse about it."

"Then don't say stupid stuff. And what makes you think I'm judging you when I don't even know who you are anymore?" I glance down at his dirty boots next to the lounge. "It's ... well, ever since Mum died, you've drunk yourself stupid." I let out a sigh and lift my gaze. "I miss her too, you know. But I don't carry on like this and get drunk every night because of it."

Bill turns his head and looks out the darkened window. "Well, we all can't be as good as Toby now can we?" Gradually, his eyes find their way back, stopping first at my chest and then up at my face. "You might judge me, brother, but you don't know what it was like. You don't know how it felt to wrap her lifeless body into a quilt and bury her like a mongrel dog." He swallows. I watch the tears develop in his eyes. "So don't tell me how to act when you don't understand." He shifts in the lounge and looks back to the window. He takes a drink.

As I stand there, it hadn't occurred to me that he might feel this way. The memory of him carrying our mother's body, of him laying her down in the hole, of him covering her with dirt, plays back through my mind.

"She was our mum, Toby, and I buried her like a ..." He swallows. "It's because of those rich bastards and their cemetery. I should've tried harder. I should have listened to you. Listened to Picker. He told me to wait until he saw the priest." He turns his face, and I notice a stray tear travelling down over his cheek. "Instead, I just accepted it for what it was. I'm the one who decided to put her out there, and I'm the one who has to live with that." He swipes the side of his face with the back of his hand.

"It affects me too, Bill."

"Well, you don't seem to show it."

"What? Because I don't drink and wallow in my pain?"

"No, I'm not saying that. I'm the one who carried her body out to that hole." Face thunderous, he thumps his fist into his chest. "I'm the one who covered her with soil. It was me, but I guess you couldn't figure that out 'coz you're too busy grieving over a girl. She's gone, you know. She ain't ever coming back. I loved her too. She left me as well, but you don't see me pining on that, do ya, brother?"

As soon as the words break away from his lips, his expression closes off. It's as if he's given away too much information.

For the moment, all I can do is look at him in astonishment. "What do you mean you loved her?"

He looks away and avoids answering the question. Instead, he takes another swig of beer.

"Just answer the question, Bill!" I stare hard at him. "We all loved her, but I don't understand why you would ache for her." He shifts in the lounge and edges his eyes back to me. "What are you not telling me, Bill?"

He remains stubbornly silent, and then, as if my harsh stare prods the truth out of him, he slams the bottle down onto the table and lifts both hands. "Okay, I loved her too. Is that what you want to hear? I fell in love with my brother's girl. There—I said it." He lets out a long sigh. "Are ya happy now?"

I retreat a few steps, struggling to decipher exactly what he said. Then it all comes racing back. He was always there, hanging around when Hildy was at the house. If Sam or I poked fun at her, he would defend her. The night at her parent's house, he wouldn't leave. And the way he held her hand. And that last embrace. The gates—he continued to check them long after she had gone. How could I have been so ignorant that I didn't see that? The concept is almost laughable. Almost. Except it is true. I stand there three feet away from him, stunned, with my mouth open. "I c-can't believe any of ..." Feeling betrayed, I swallow loudly. "How could you, Bill? Brothers don't do that to each other. I can't understand you." Betrayed, I turn away from him and move towards the door.

Bill calls after me. "You need to forget that rich bitch, brother. She treated you the same way those arseholes treated our mother. When are you going to realise you meant nothing to her?"

"What?" I snap my head around. I'm furious. "I meant nothing to her?" I repeat his words dumbly.

"All you do is sit here day after day waiting for her to come back." He licks his lips. "And where is she? She's gone! Don't you think if she were coming back, she would have already been here? Well?"

For a few seconds, the air in the room feels suffocating. His words, which I know are the truth, cut right through me.

"She didn't care about you. She didn't even have the decency to let you know where she was going. Get it through that thick skull—you meant nothing to her. She's gone. Probably moved on to someone else, doing all those sexual things you wished she had done to you."

"Shut up!" My fists clench at my side. The fury burns in my belly. "Don't you dare talk about her that way! You shut the hell up, Bill!"

"Jesus, Toby, get over it. You're the oldest virgin I know. It's pathetic that you sit here waiting for her to come back. I'm embarrassed for you." He leans forward and snatches another bottle from the table and pops off the cap. "I think you should see Sylvie. She'll take care of that for you. She'll show you a good time." He lifts the bottle up as if making a toast. "Trust me. I can guarantee you won't be thinking about Hildy anymore."

"How can you say that about Sylvie?"

He mumbles something, but I can't make it out.

"I thought you cared for Sylvie."

He looks up and glares hard. A muscle ticks at the side of his jaw. "No. Sylvie's only been my distraction because the person I truly want, I can't have. She left years ago. I suppose you should be thankful that she did because that's the only reason that stopped me from going after her."

A burning rage hisses through me. Every word adds fuel to the fire.

"Go see Sylvie," he suggests again. "She'll teach you a few dirty tricks. I promise you won't dwell on that rich bitch anymore. I certainly don't."

Blood boiling, I launch myself across the table. Bottles scatter over the floor. My hand presses against his throat. The momentum knocks him back into the lounge. I lean over, shove my face down into his, and glare at him with bulging eyes. His hot, intoxicated breath settles on my skin. "If you ever speak of Hildy that way again, I'm gonna hurt you." My pulse thumps wildly. "Do you understand? Tell me you understand, Bill!"

A cruel sneer appears. His eyes bore straight into mine. "Maybe I should have been with Hildy. At least that way I could have protected her."

And there it is—the truth—after all this time. His words carry more damage than a physical punch. I draw my fist back, ready to strike.

"Come on, do it!" His eyes glow. "You don't have the guts to do it."

It is only then that I realise he wants me to react. He's baiting me. He could always get a reaction out of me with his "one-up" games. And still, today, I let him fire me up. I slow my breathing, allowing myself time to think. He wants me to lash out and punish him for all the things he has done.

"See? Told ya you couldn't do it. You're a coward." He sucks in a deep breath. "Not enough balls to follow through on anything. How pathetic are you? I'm embarrassed to call you my brother."

As soon as I loosen my grip from around his throat, his whole face alters. His eyes drop to my chest with the realisation that I'm not playing his game anymore.

A moment later, he lifts his hand and shoves me away.

"Get off me." He slumps further into the lounge. "Get out and let me sleep."

Eyeing him, I step back a few paces. Fate had pushed both our lives into a path we never planned, and in the process transformed us into people neither one of us can recognise.

"What are you looking at?" He spits the words out at me.

I ignore him by picking up the overturned table and collecting the bottles from the floor. His eyes continue to watch me. I half expect him to add some smart-arse comment, but he remains quiet.

I give one last look before I turn my back on him and walk out the door.

15

That night, I can't sleep. No matter what I do, I cannot throw Bill's words out of my head. The guilt takes me down a familiar path. After all these years, he's finally said it. He thinks I'm responsible for what happened to Hildy. Every day, I've tortured myself by asking that exact question. Now to have him say the words only affirms the truth. I didn't try hard enough to protect her. I wasn't strong enough. Not in the way I needed to be. The chaos of that day has choked my life, and it has never been the same. Now I second-guess everything, including myself.

I close my eyes. My mind drifts in many directions. The anguish of missing Hildy comes once again. It always returns in those silent, vulnerable moments. It feels as if a part of me is not here anymore. How does Bill know that I've been so broken without her? Has it been that obvious?

The anger comes in as I think about our conversation. Who the hell is Bill to say I have issues? He's the one with the problem. I'm not a drunk or a massive pain in the arse. He should look at himself before pointing his finger at me. He's the one who sleeps on the lounge. He's the one who's drinking himself into an early grave.

I roll onto my side and peer out through the window. With the silvery moonlight washing in, the glass pane reflects a man staring back at me—a man I don't recognise. I study him, paying particular attention to the way he has changed over the years: the thick facial hair that covers his jaw-line, his prominent forehead and deep-set eyes, and the slightly wider nose. I think about my mother and wonder what she would have thought about this man and the life he has adopted for himself. A wave of shame washes over me. The person that I have become goes against every life lesson my mother taught. Her efforts have been lost on me, lost on Bill. All her struggles to give us a better life should at least mean something. Anything. Embarrassed, I roll away.

All of a sudden, her words come into my mind. "There is beauty in everything, even at times when you cannot see it."

Sitting up, I shift over to the edge of the bed. Every-thing about who I was—that happy young kid, the way I once viewed the world—is slowly being erased. I need to find myself again. I need to remember what it was like to be that youthful boy. To capture it all back before the toxins seep further in and blotch that little boy's existence right out of my soul. I need to remember how to be me.

I ruffle my hands back through my hair, not knowing the answers. Where will I go? I have no one out there in this world except my father. And I have no intentions of ever seeing him again. I couldn't care less if he's alive or not. He's dead to me anyway.

Only yesterday Picker told me that the O'Malley boy from down the road is leaving to enlist in the War. Maybe I should join the boys in the Pacific. At least that way, I'll have somewhere to go.

I plop my body back onto the bed and close my eyes. Once again, Hildy's image comes into my head. It doesn't matter how many times I try to remove it; it always survives unchanged. I lie there. The silence is suffocating.

In the morning, I get up and move about the house. As I walk, my brain shuffles through the many ways in which I can explain to Bill my decision to leave. I stop in the open doorway, lean my hip against the doorjamb, and study Bill, who is passed out on the lounge. His face is gaunt. There's drool oozing down from the side of his mouth and pooling into his beard. His thin, frail body and bony hands now only suggest weakness. He is no longer the brother I remember. Instead, he's been tucked away and now exists only in my memory. I do not wish to know this stranger here in front of me. If our mother could see us now for who we are, she would be so disappointed that we have lost our identities. Neither one of us is capable of fixing the other. We are both too broken to even try. The one thing I do know is that I cannot stay here any longer. I have already witnessed my brother fade almost beyond recognition. I refuse to watch him die a slow, agonising death at the hands of a bottle. Too many people over the years have left me. I will not stick around and wait for him to do the same.

Later that afternoon, I finish up my final shift on Picker's farm. As I walk home, I rehearse the words that I will say to Bill. But the moment I step up onto the front porch and hear Bill snoring, the words vanish from my mind. I yank open the door and move into the room, purposely letting the door bang behind me. A thick, gravelly wheeze continues to roll in and out of Bill's throat.

On the way over to him, I collect two empty bottles from the floor and set them down on the table. "Bill, wake up. I have something to tell you." I tap the side of his leg. "Bill!"

He doesn't stir.

I peer down at the table and snatch up a half-empty bottle. With one quick movement, I turn the bottle upside down. The ale pours down over his face.

Instantly, he springs to life, gasping and spluttering. He jerks back in the lounge, wiping the wetness from his eyes. "Hey! What the bloody hell did you do that for?"

"Because I need to tell you something."

"Well, ya didn't have to do that." He pushes his hands back through his wet hair. "You could have just woke me up like a normal person."

"Yeah, right? I didn't think of that one." I roll my eyes at him.

"Well, go on—what's so bloody important that you had to do that?"

"I'm leaving tomorrow."

"Leaving?" He swallows and shifts in the lounge. "Where are ya going?"

"I'm going to sign up."

"Sign up for what?"

"You do know there is a war going on?" My eyes lower down to the ale dripping from his beard. "I've decided I am gonna sign up."

"Are you serious?" He shifts over to the edge of the lounge. "What about your job? What's Picker gonna say?"

"I've already told him."

"And what did the old bastard say about that?"

"He was fine. He was sorry to see me go, but he understood the reason."

"So, what? You're leaving, no matter what I think?"

"Yes. I'm only telling you because I thought you should know. Not that you would even realise I've gone."

"If you're going, then I'm going too."

"No. No way. Absolutely not."

"Why?" His voice rises.

"Look at yourself, Bill." I fight to hold his impenetrable stare. "How in the hell are you gonna be able to sign up when you can't even drag your arse off the lounge. The only time you ever get up is when you're looking for sex or another bottle to guzzle. You're no good for anything at the moment."

"Brother," he cuts in, holding up his finger, "I don't think Sylvie would agree with you on that one."

A tiny chuckle snorts out of my mouth, easing the moment a little. I sigh and sit in the armchair opposite. "Bill, you can't come. If there were a way, then I would let you, but there isn't." I cast my eyes down to the table. "Besides, you wouldn't want to miss out on all of this, now would you?" I raise my head.

He stares back at me. He's in no mood for a joke.

"Toby, I realise I haven't been there for you lately." His gaze slides down to the floor.

"Years, Bill. It's been years."

He glances up.

I see the disappointment on his face. "I know. I know, and I'm sorry. I let you down. I've let Mum down." He draws in a breath. His eyes water. "I made a promise to Mum years ago to always keep you safe. I've done a great job with it, hey?" He forces a smile.

Something about the way he has said this showed his vulnerability. It was as if he had no control over his actions or the way he had changed over the years.

"There are so many things that go through my head. No matter how hard I try, I can't shake them." Bill taps the side of his skull with his fingers. "They sit right here, day after day, taunting me. I can't talk to anyone about it. Not even my baby brother. So, I get drunk because it's easier to deal with it. Easier to forget all the awful things I have done."

"But until you deal with them, they won't go away."

"But they will. If you let me go with you, I will be better. I promise."

"I don't see how—"

"I'll be doing something different. I won't be here." He turns his head and stares out the window. "Just being here every day reminds me of it. All of it." He remains silent until his eyes find their way back. "Please don't leave me, brother. Everyone leaves me. You're all the family I've got."

I look over to the brother who helped raise me. My heart aches as I witness his honestly, as I think about the burdens he carries. I can still see the events of our mother's death unfolding before my eyes, as plainly as if three years haven't passed. I know what he is feeling—the doubt, the compulsion, the blame, that sense of guilt nibbling away on your soul.

After all these years, I now see the similarities. We are the same. Bill is like a mirror reflecting me. Our paths have run parallel to each other; the only difference is that his veered off into alcoholism, and mine turned into isolation.

I put the empty bottle down on the table because I don't know what to say. How did we get here? How did we get to a place where neither one of us can talk about our problems to the other? Throughout our lives, we have shared everything. We've had a bond that could never be broken.

"I beg you, brother, please take me with you." He sighs and rubs his hand across his chest. "I promise to try harder and be there for you." Tears come to his eyes. "I can't have you leave me like everyone else has."

I shake my head. "Bill, you need to sort yourself out first."

"Yes, I do. And I understand why you want to leave, but I need to go for the same reasons." His expression tightens as he wrestles the tears. "If I don't go, then this place will eventually kill me."

Turning my head, I stare out the window, but I don't really see anything through it. My first impulse is to walk from the room, but I can't do that, not after he has opened up to me. I take in a deep breath and slowly blow it out. "I'm leaving at dawn if you want to come. But you better be awake because I'm not coming to find you." The second the words leave my mouth, I regret them.

"Yes. Yes. Thank you, brother. You won't have to wake me in the morning. I'll be ready. You'll see."

I retreat, sidestepping a few empty bottles. I move toward the door, and just as I'm about to step through, Bill yells out from behind.

"Brother!"

I halt and glance back over my shoulder.

"Thank you. I promise I won't let you down."

I shrug it off. "Just take a shower. You stink. And shave off that awful beard. You look like an old man."

"I still look better than you."

"Yeah, whatever. You tell yourself that." I smirk as I step out of the room.

16

Early the next morning when I slip out into the kitchen, I find Bill already sitting at the end of the table. I stop and take a good look at him. His face is clean shaven. Years of alcohol abuse have left his facial features gaunt and unhealthy looking. His once-prominent jawline and thick neck appear to have wasted away. But it's my brother, or the aura of the brother I used to know.

"Well, well," he says with a cheeky smile. "I thought for a minute there I'd have to wake you up."

"Is that so?"

I'm halfway across the room when the heat from the stove hits me. "You've done it?" I turn around, my eyebrows furrowed in bewilderment. "You did the fire."

"It's no big deal." He bounces it off, lifting his shoulders. "It's just a fire."

But to me, it is a huge deal. It is progress in the right direction. The former Bill that I assumed had fled is slowly oozing in. Smiling, I give a slight nod. Maybe this is the start Bill needs. Who knows? Maybe in a couple of days, we will feel like our old selves again.

While I make breakfast, Bill sits quietly at the table, watching me potter around the room.

Forty minutes later, after eating our meals and packing our satchels, I meet Bill in the hallway, and collectively we make our way through the house. As I glance around, I seek out one perfect memory to cling onto. Instead of striking a happy childhood recollection, all I seem to observe is everything I've lost.

I push open the front door and step out of the house. My thoughts are scattered everywhere as a pandemonium of emotion sweeps through me. It's my soul mourning the end of my old life, followed by excitement for a wonderful new beginning. Bill follows me out through the doorway and then walks across the front porch. As I take hold of the doorknob, I give one last look around the room. A feeling of such sadness washes over me.

"Are you having second thoughts?" asks Bill, watching me. He readjusts his satchel on his shoulder.

I toss a quick look at him before closing the door as if his comment somehow registered the truth. "No." I add, shaking my head. I turn around to find him still standing there, studying me. "I just had one last look, that's all." I knew it was pointless to talk to Bill about my feelings after I'd made such a strong argument yesterday about leaving.

As I walk past him, he keeps his eyes on me to see if I'm

telling the truth. Then he quickly catches up. Together we move down the front steps.

"Bill, do you think we'll ever come back here?"

"I don't know, but I'm happy we're leaving."

Turning left, we wander over to the rose garden. We each snap off a single red rose. Side by side, we approach the old gum tree, stopping at the base of our mother's grave. In our hearts, we both hold off announcing our last goodbyes. Coming together, we arrange our roses in the soft grass under the tree. It's a simple gesture, but it's one that is still filled with such raw emotion, knowing that this will be our last gift to our mother. Bill doesn't stay long. He's the first one to walk away. It's an automatic reaction to the guilt he must be feeling. I wait a little longer. Bending down on one knee, I clear away a few twigs and dead leaves. For the most part, I will take with me the memory of those wonderful days when I found her sewing in the kitchen. With a quick glance around the area, I see Bill waiting for me. Standing, I give one last look at the grave, and with a heavy heart, I turn my back on my mother and walk away.

As Bill waits, his face is tight and his jaw is clenched.

I take a deep breath. "You ready?" I say, stepping up next to him.

He nods. His face seems to relax.

After we've walked the full length of the drive, Bill secures the gate, and together we stand there eyeing the old home, letting go of the only life we have ever known.

By mid-morning, Bill's pace has slowed. He's struggling to keep up. Stuck in the middle of nowhere, I pause and glance back over my shoulder. And even though Bill lags behind a good twenty yards, fear jolts through me as I take in his image. He's hunched over. Sweat has covered his entire body. His messy hair is saturated and now clings to the sides of his face. The way he sucks the air into his lungs confirms he's in real trouble.

"Bill!" I race back. "Here, let me help you."

He looks up. Sweat dribbles from the end of his nose. "Bill, are you okay?" I reach my hand out to help him.

He slaps it away. "Get away from me. I don't need your help. I just need to take a break."

"Okay. Then, give me your bag. It looks heavy." I extend my arm out.

He twists away. "No!" He cradles the satchel close to his side. "Just leave it alone. I can carry it myself."

"Bill, don't be so stubborn. Just give it to me." I snatch the strap from his shoulder. At lightning speed, he snatches it back.

"Why are you like this?"

"Like what?"

"You're being an arse right now."

"Just leave my bag alone, and we won't have a problem." A muscle tics at the side of his jaw. That's always been my cue to leave it alone, for the moment anyway.

I step back and survey the area. The countryside stretches before us, rising and falling like a dry wave. The odd tree dots the land. To the right, there's nothing but vast dry land with the occasional thorny bush. To my relief, over to the left are the few lonely trees offering the only shade. That will have to do.

I spin back around and forcefully thread my arm in around his sweaty back.

"What are you doing?" He snaps, trying once again to push me away.

"Do you want a break or not? Now shut up and just let me help. We need to walk over there." I point over to the trees, which are at least a hundred yards away.

He lifts his face. His eyes dart back and forth between me and the trees. Deciding the distance is a tad too far, he raises his arm up over my neck. "Okay, but I can carry my own bag."

But the second I slip my arm in around his back, he stumbles and his head rolls back. I push my shoulder in under his armpit to support his body weight. The dizziness sets in. Now he's disorientated. He can't move. With all the effort and strength I can muster, I hoist him up off the ground. Even though he's half the size he once was, I still find it difficult to carry him comfortably. Drawing in a long breath, I glance up to the trees and start the hike.

Bill grumbles all the way. From time to time, I have to pause to shift him into a more comfortable position in my arms.

When we finally arrive in the shade, I settle his exhausted body down onto the ground. In an instant, he stretches out onto his back and drags the satchel possessively in towards his hip. I sit down next to him. Retrieving the water bottle from my bag, I unscrew the lid. He coughs and splutters for air. I offer him the first drink.

"I don't need it." He stares up at me. The torment on his face is visible.

"Yes you do. Now take it or I'll ram it down your bloody throat."

He remains stubborn.

"Bill, you need water. Don't fight me on this one."

"I will in a minute." He closes his eyes. "Just let me catch my breath first."

"What time did you get up this morning?" I say, looking out over the countryside. I take a sip of water.

"I didn't."

"What do you mean you didn't?" I take another drink.

"It's exactly what I said. I didn't go to bed." Interlocking his fingers, he rests them down on top of his chest and readjusts his head into a more relaxed position. "I had to go to Sylvie and get my goodbye present."

My head snaps around. "Are you serious, Bill? And I suppose you were drinking there too."

"It's the last time, brother. I promise."

"You know, something told me I was making a huge mistake bringing you with me. But no, I didn't listen." I whip my head around and glare out at the view. "What the hell is wrong with you? Are you trying to kill yourself? Cause if you are, then I will just leave you here and let you do it. All I can say is that you're a bloody idiot, and I'm an even bigger one for letting you—" I stop talking the moment Bill snores. Glancing sideways, I discover he's fallen asleep. "That's just great!" I add, throwing the water bottle back into the bag. I stretch my legs out in front and yank a piece of stalky grass from the ground, placing it between my teeth. How could I have been so stupid? Why did I think he would change?

My gaze quickly shifts to the satchel he still clutches under his arm. What does he have in there that he doesn't want me to see? I push up onto my knees, and with extreme care, I pull the bag free from his protective arm. Opening the flap, the first item I see on the top is a scrunched-up shirt. I reach in and pull it out. There, standing tall like an army of tiny soldiers are six bottles of ale. The sight of those bottlenecks hits me like a fist to the gut. "What the hell, Bill?" I fling the shirt down onto the ground and sit back, running my hands through my hair, now unsure of what to do.

Silently I sit there, lost somewhere amongst my thoughts, thinking of his betrayal versus the loyalty that I

have for him. Shifting my head, I study him for the longest
time, knowing that there is a dark pit inside him now
that has all the control. It demands to be the master no
matter the cost. The reality of losing him hurts more than I
care to admit. But I know I have to face the truth. I can't lie
any longer. He is lost to me.

A huge lump appears in the back of my throat. All
our years together come down to this. What will I do
with him? Do I leave him here or do I take him back to
the house? I picture him sitting on the lounge all alone, still
punishing himself for everything he has done. No matter
how furious he makes me, I know in my heart I cannot
send him back to that house and then just leave. For that
will make me no different than my father. The life we have
known has definitely ended. For the very first time in my
life, I wonder if our mother gave us unreal expectations
about life, because look at who we have become. We are both
running from the ghosts of our pasts. Our lives now seem
pointless. There is nothing but guilt, regret, and suffering. All
I know is, for us to move on, the negativity has to stop
today. But how? How can I help him? What's gonna make him
want to change?

I turn my head and snatch a bottle from the bag, pop
the top, and tip the contents out. Golden, glistening ale
trickles down over the dark soil, twisting and curving like
a deadly snake. When one bottle is empty, I grab another,
and then another and another until there is nothing left.

With all six bottles empty, I carefully repack the
satchel and slide it back in under Bill's arm. He doesn't
stir. I sit back and breathe a sigh of relief.

As the night deepens, I stretch out onto my back and
stare up at the countless stars above me. Nothing from

my old life can touch me here. I'm free. Knowing that, I feel the tears form at the sides of my eyes and slide down my face. In some way, the crying feels right. With every hour comes peace, and with every breath, a sense of calmness. All I want is to be happy. I can't imagine ever going back to the house. It is late when sleep finally finds me.

The next morning, as dawn breaks through the darkness, I wake. Still, there is no change in Bill. Now I begin to worry.

In the hours that follow, the heat bounces off the land causing an illusion of wavering landscape. The wind picks up, scattering dried leaves and debris in around us. Waiting for him to wake is torture. Throughout the day, I ration out tiny portions of water and feed it to Bill, and a little to myself, but only when I needed it. To pass the time, I think about my father. I think about how things might have worked out differently if only he had stayed.

At around four in the afternoon, Bill's eyes flutter open.

"Good, you're awake." I get up onto my feet. "I've been so worried about you, Bill."

He doesn't say anything. He just shuffles up onto his elbow, pries open the bag, and removes the shirt. The moment he sees that the bottles are empty, his whole face changes. "No!" He glares up at me. "What the hell have you done?" He grabs one empty bottle after the other and frantically tosses them aside. When the bag is empty, he lifts his head. His face is full of rage.

I won't write the colourful language he uses on me that day. But when Bill's crawling in the ash, he is pitiful. I can sense the pain lurking through his body, and within the hour, after all the moaning and cursing and bitching about what I'd done, his body takes over. He pukes over and over until there is nothing left to bring up.

I can't do anything except offer him some water. And as I do that, he doesn't hold back the harsh words.

As the hours play out, he begins to sweat. Every strand of hair clings together; his sweat-drenched shirt clings tightly to his torso. And then, as the hours go by, in come the shakes.

At this point, I am so conflicted. I'm not sure of what to do. Do I race back and find help or stay here just in case he needs me? But the choice is soon taken out of my hands when the sun slips down behind the horizon, spreading the last rays of light over the land. As bird-shaped silhouettes fly off into the distance, I stay with him. Gradually, the night crawls in.

For most of the night and into the next morning, I catch myself checking on him just to make sure he's still breathing. My emotions have gone haywire.

The next day comes in, and still there is no change in Bill. I sit there. The wait is excruciating.

By the fourth day, I feel reassured when I glance across to check on him and find him awake, watching me.

"Hey, Bill." I stand and grab my water bottle. "How are you feeling? You look a little worse for wear."

"I still look better than you."

I look down at him and grin. "Not possible."

On the fifth day, we walk most of the day towards Sydney, occasionally stopping to rest or to fill up our water bottles. Bill's smart-arse attitude comes out. Often I find him having a dig just to tease me or wrapping his arm up around my neck in a headlock the way he did when we were kids. I hated it back then, and still loath it, but I say nothing about it because I have my brother back again.

As the miles slip away, Bill passes the time by telling a few jokes. And I will admit, after all the worry over the last few days, it is good to laugh again, especially with him.

Neither one of us mentions the bottles of alcohol or the life we are walking away from. I suppose we don't want to pop our happy bubble. Just being there with Bill, walking next to him, laughing, makes me feel as if time has evaporated and spun us back to our youth when I found it comforting to have him at my side.

By the time we arrive in Sydney, we've been on the road for seven days. After that, we are given our uniforms, our rifles, and little basic training. Then we're on our way to Papua New Guinea.

17

It is said among the many few who have returned home from the war that our stories should not be shared. I also avoid talking about my time there. But I do want to share the two occasions that helped shaped the course of my life.

Nevertheless, you may have heard something about the Pacific War. Forgive me if I'm repeating what you already know, but I think it will help you understand my story better.

War is evil. I only wish I'd known that before I left. I didn't understand what I was running into; I was so determined to go. My world changed and not for the better. It was as if I'd been snatched from a world saturated with sunshine and dumped into complete darkness.

Every day there it rained, and every day we'd plod through the mud—muck that was so deep, it could swallow you whole.

Week after week, our unit would roam up and down the hillsides, always on edge, waiting for the moment when the enemy would pop up its ugly head. It wasn't just the enemy we had to contend with, but the mosquitoes too. They were so full of blood, they were double their usual size. Over time, we developed sores over our legs that would never heal because of the germ-infested mud.

At night, we would sleep on the sides of the hills. We would have to anchor ourselves to a tree just to stop from sliding down the hill during the night. If we didn't, we would certainly wake a good many yards from where we first started. In those quiet moments, Hildy would always find her way into my dreams. She was what I held onto. In those dark moments, she brought with her a light I needed to survive.

Honestly, I'm not sure what I thought would change by going there. I really hadn't thought it through. I'd made one stupid split decision that would forever scar my life. From the moment I arrived, I wanted to go home. It depressed me, and the more that death plucked off the people around me, the stronger I clung to the memories of home. Many times, I imagined myself sitting on the back verandah watching the sky split, breathing in the sweet scent of wildflowers in the breeze.

Bill, on the other hand, thrived. I know that sounds bizarre given that environment, but the war sorted him out. I suppose his mind was focused on current-day issues and not filled with judgements of the past. Over time, he settled into a new routine with no complications. As the weeks increased, the other soldiers would assemble around the two of us just to hear his jokes and funny stories.

He started smoking, much to my disappointment, but I presume it was a way for him to deal with the alcohol cravings.

From the moment we arrived on that island, something had changed between us. A new brotherly bond was forged. Something within him had resurfaced, bringing with it a more protective, caring role. I am now convinced the only reason he wanted to come with me was to honour the promise he made to our mother. Because he never let me out of his sight.

Now that you have all that information, let me tell you about this one particular day.

The raindrops are so fat that visibility is down to only a yard in front of us. As we manoeuvre up the side of the sodden hill, Bill, once again, taps on my left shoulder. I've become so accustomed to the pats. I know they are for his benefit mainly, to ease his mind so he's aware I'm still standing at his side.

With the last of the light fading, we settle down on the side of the hill for the night.

I pull my boot from the sucking mud. It's a tiring process, but it's one we need to do to stay ahead of the enemy. I hear Bill's voice.

"Brother, come over here."

Through the misty rain, I find him standing in front of two trees. I make my way over, tossing my backpack down onto the ground. Giving my back a good stretch, I look up at the cloudy sky above me, letting the rain wash over my face. I sit down next to Bill as I bring my mind back to what I am supposed to be focusing on. I remember the first time I slept on the wet soggy ground. It was kind of strange, but now that I've been doing it for so long, it seems normal to me.

Bill pulls out a tobacco tin from his pocket and rolls a cigarette.

As I lean back against the tree, he speaks.

"Do you want one?"

"No, I don't think so. But you already knew that."

"Yeah, I know, but you might want to toughen up a bit."

I drop my head back against the tree. "What? Do you think smoking makes you look tough?"

"Nah, not really, but ya gotta admit, it does kinda make me look cool."

"If anything, it makes you look stupid." I laugh and shake my head. "You're delusional."

"Say what you want, brother, but I know you want to be just like me."

"Yeah, as I said—delusional."

He laughs out loud, sticks the end of the cigarette between his lips, strikes a match, and draws back on it.

I turn my head away from him. All around me, cigarettes glow in the darkness as soldiers take advantage of the break. Night-time is the worst for me. All my senses become amplified because I know the enemy is out there. A movement in the shadows makes me paranoid. The foliage swaying under the rain is enough to make me hold my breath, make my heart thump wildly in my chest. And no matter how many times it has happened, I can't seem to switch it off. It's as if my body now needs the adrenalin racing through my veins so I can survive.

For the next hour, Bill and I sit there, sopping up the rain. Another movement. I catch myself shuddering as my eyes continue to play those cruel tricks.

Then, from out of nowhere, the rain just stops. I stand and let out a long sigh as I look up to see the clouds separate. Through the gap, I seize a peek of the glittering stars. It's the first time I've seen them since being here.

Into the silence, I hear Bill's voice. "It's amazing, isn't it, brother?"

I blink as I bring my mind back. "You mean the stars?"

"No," Bill says, frowning. He points forward. "Look over there."

My gaze follows his finger. There, across the gully, the enemy shifts down the hillside. Each soldier seems to carry a lantern of some sort. The view is beautiful. It's mesmerising. Peaceful. It's like watching a giant glow worm wriggle its way down the side of the hill. At that moment, my senses seem to relax as the blanket of pure beauty and calm falls over me. The war has gone. The world shows me once again how beautiful it can be. It is then I understand my mother's words.

Bill clears his throat. "Brother, I never said sorry for what I did."

I turn my head to find Bill is standing so close. "You're not drinking again are you?"

"No." He chuckles. "I'm serious. I never said thank you. You could have just left me there, but you didn't. You brought me back to life, and I will never forget that. Thank you."

"I did it because of what you said."

"What did I say?"

"You said we only have each other."

"It's true. I also need to say sorry for what I said about Hildy. It was never your fault for what happened to her." He swallows. "I just said it because I knew it would hurt. I wasn't myself. I sort of get it though."

"Get what?"

"Why you miss her. Once you meet someone like her, no one else matches up. She's irreplaceable. I didn't want to love her, brother. I tried so hard not to, but no matter what I did it still happened."

"None of that matters now. She's gone."

"So you forgive me?" He wraps his arm up around my neck, twisting my body down, holding me in a headlock.

"I won't if you don't let me go." I try to push him away.

"All right then." He releases his grip.

I straighten up. "Do you know how annoying that is?"

"Arrr ... Yeah." He grins and turns his attention back to the view.

That night, I sleep soundly for the first time since arriving. Something has shifted in me. When I wake the following morning, my outlook on the world has altered. I finally let go of trying to control everything. I realise life is full of beautiful surprises, and they show up when you least expect them.

Three months later, when night vanishes in the new morning sun, we wake to the noise of continuous gunfire. By the time I roll over onto my stomach, Bill's already wrapped his body around me.

"Keep still, brother, until we can find a way out."

The bullets rain down over us. Holding the brim of my helmet, I tuck my head back into my shoulders turtle-like and pray desperately for this frightful moment to be over with.

Suddenly, the ground rumbles beneath me. Soldiers scream out in pain. There's another explosion and then another. Underneath Bill, I hold my breath in my lungs. My whole body shakes in a way I can't control. Through the deafening blasts, Bill's voice somehow finds its way into my ears.

"Hang in there, brother. We'll find a way out soon."

We huddle there together for what seems like an eternity. Then, on a whim, Bill gets to his feet and pulls me up by the shirt. With our feet pounding on the earth, we run. Darting our way through the foliage, we veer right and then left, narrowly dodging the bullets that rain down over us like a meteor shower.

From somewhere behind, I hear another blood-curdling scream. Twenty feet in front of us, a bomb explodes. Dozens of soldiers are thrown into the air like worthless, unwanted dolls. Fear prompts me to flee. I pivot off to the right.

From behind Bill screams out. "Go, go, go!"

As my rifle smacks against the side of my hip, I twist and weave my way through the thick jungle grass. Unexpectedly, my feet slide. I drop face first into the slush. A second later, Bill snaps me up. When my legs recover, we race on. All around us, soldiers lie face down in pools of their own blood. It's an image that will stay with me over the years and one I will never forget.

When we're through the worst of it, I slow and glance back over my shoulder, only to find the person standing behind me is not Bill.

I catch my breath and search for him.

He's not there.

I turn to the person behind. "Have you seen Bill? "

"Nah, sorry, mate. I haven't."

The silence is unsettling for a second as I stand there. Fear sits in my body as my brain tries to figure out where he is. To the left, I spot a handful of Bill's mates lighting up their cigarettes. I examine every face in the group. He's still not there.

An intense ball of emotion edges its way into the back of my throat as I start thinking the worst.

Time passes in slow motion. My breath comes out in tiny spurts with the rising panic. For the next two hours, I gawk at every face that walks by.

Knowing that I can no longer put off checking the wounded, and lastly the dead, I stand and make my way over to the hospital. The smell of death looms in the air.

After looking at every wounded and mangled soldier and the immobile face of each corpse, I feel numb. I stare at the ground mutely as I come to face the only possible truth left. He's dead. His body must still be out there on the jungle floor. My entire world shuts down. The fog closes in. It's suffocating. The severe pain hacks me apart. Tears gash in my eyes. I try to suck in a breath as the sadness creeps in, flooding me right through to the bones. I cry, stilted at first in an attempt to hide the grief from all those around me. But the overcoming wave of emotion crushes me. I collapse onto my knees as my defences give way. Every inch of my body is racked. Every raw sob finds its way out of me as I grieve for the big brother I have lost.

Twenty-Seven

18

Four years and fifty-five days. That's how long it's been since I've seen my childhood home. I can't believe I'm standing here looking at it once again.

The gate has fallen away, the hinges too rusty to hold it up. I pick it up and move it off to one side before walking down the driveway. As I walk, I keep my eyes forward, taking in my surroundings. Every part of this house is etched in my mind, but today, it looks a little different to the way I remember. Maybe age has transformed both of us.

Up ahead, the grass of the overgrown lawns rustles in the breeze. On the roof, a rusty sheet of tin lifts with the wind as if it's waving to me, welcoming me home. The old shed next to the house is scarred from the weather; half its roof is now missing.

When I stand in front of the house, I notice the porch steps have almost rotted away.

Sliding my hands into my pockets, I turn my head sidewards and take in the old majestic gum. This tree holds a lifetime of memories for me. How I loved those days when Bill and I would spend hours climbing its low hanging branches. It is a place where Hildy and I would sometimes sit for hours in the shade, talking. Now it will always be my mother's final resting place.

The southerly breeze picks up. I am bombarded with the sweet scent of wildflowers. I close my eyes and smile as the memories trickle in. There's a strange sense of normality as I stand here now. I know who I am. My stories are sprayed all over these walls.

I open my eyes with a sense of belonging. Never again will I be tempted to leave this place, to find something better. There is nothing better out there. I want to recall everything from my past. I wish to hang onto those beautiful moments with all the people I loved. I want to keep them safe within my heart.

I move up the weather-beaten steps, walk across the front porch, push open the creaking door, and enter the house. I am aware I am no longer that confused young boy who used to live here. He is long gone. He has been scarred by the worst that human nature has to offer. He has seen unspeakable things that only a war can show a person. If I could go back in time to tell that young kid to stay and deal with his demons, I would. For the alternative is far worse than he could ever imagine. War is not the answer he was looking for. It will forever change him in ways he never thought possible. And he will never be the same.

Sidestepping a few bottles on the floor, I move across the room and pull back the heavy curtains. Light explodes into the room. With one hand shoved in my pocket, I glance around. I take in the six empty bottles resting on the table. It's a forgotten recollection of part of my brother I don't care to remember. In my mind, he will always be laughing and joking.

Draped on the back of the lounge is the last quilt my mother ever made. I walk over and trace my fingers across her perfect stitches. My mind pops up an image of her sitting in the kitchen sewing.

It is now time to open the windows to air the house, to allow all the ghosts from my past to escape. I can still feel my mother and brother here, and I will always draw comfort from knowing that, but it's time to move on. Time to stop dwelling on the past. It is time to hold my head up high and think about the future, so my new life can begin. I've accepted those losses for what they are. I understand that, in the darkest of times, we can still turn everything around. My brother showed me that.

Walking from room to room, I can't figure out why I'm so surprised to find it looks exactly the same. The old furniture, the trinkets, the photographs. It seems so long ago when my family members were here to appreciate them.

I move down through the shadowed hall and stop outside my bedroom. The floorboards creak under my feet. It's a soothing reminder of the life I once had. I nudge open the door, and just as I'm about to step into the room, a voice yells out to me.

"Toby, are you there, mate?"

I smile at the familiarity of the voice. "Yeah, I'm here." I turn and retreat down the hall. As soon as I emerge into the front room, I see Picker peeking in through the screen. In one hand, he is holding his wide-brimmed hat, and in the other, he's clutching a few ales.

He smiles. "G'day, mate. I thought it was you walking up the road." He steps back to allow me to push open the screen. "Jeeze, it's good to see you." His eyes scan over me as I step through the doorway. "Only yesterday I thought the two of you would be home soon. I'm glad to see you're back in one piece." He slips a cold bottle of ale into my hand.

"Thanks. Yeah, it's good to be home." I walk forward and motion for us to sit down.

"Where's Bill, I didn't see him with you. Is he already here?" He tosses a look back at the door. "I grabbed him a beer, but now I come to think of it, it might not be such a good idea."

When I remain silent, he shifts his head and stares at me.

"Bill didn't make it back." I peer forward and look out over the land, my throat tightens.

"Oh, no Toby. I'm sorry. I had no idea." He shakes his head, and his bushy eyebrows furrow.

"Come on, let's take a seat and I'll catch you up." I wait for him to take a seat. "I'm not absolutely certain what happened to him. One minute he was there beside me, and then the next, he was gone." I raise the bottle up to my mouth and take a sip.

"What, he just disappeared?"

"Yep. He was killed in one of the morning attacks. It was a few years ago now. We never recovered his body. It's as if he dissolved into thin air." I swallow the lump in the back of my throat and turn to Picker to find his eyes are watching me.

"Toby, I don't know what to say. We had our differences with the whole Sylvie thing, but I thought of him as a son." His eyes glisten with tears.

"Yeah, he was embarrassed by the way he behaved. He told me that."

Picker clears his throat, and I see a tear coming.

My own eyes water, and I have to look away.

"He was a good lad."

I dart my gaze back. "No, he wasn't." I grin.

"No, you're right." Picker smiles and then lets out a chuckle. "In fact, he was a real little shit. But—" He raises a finger. "He was a hard worker, I'll give him that. He was a funny bugger. Him and his bloody stories! He could keep me entertained for days, you know. I will miss him." He holds the bottle out to make a toast. "To Bill. May he find his peace."

"To Bill."

We tap our bottles together and take a sip.

We both remain silent for a moment. Neither one of us knows what to say.

Finally, Picker says, "I see you've got some jobs to do around here." He points over to the steps with his bottle.

"Yeah. I'm surprised it's lasted this long. The steps were always bouncy and needed replacing. But the old shed surprised me. That's gonna cost a bit to fix."

"So you're gonna stay then?"

"I never should have left."

"If you need the truck to get supplies, you know where it is."

I give a warm smile. "Thanks, but I have no money at the moment."

"Just add it to my account." He takes a swig of beer.

"Yeah. I don't know about that. It wouldn't feel right owing you money."

"If you're worried about that, then just pay it back when you're ready or do a few shifts. I don't care. Your job's still there if you want it."

"I think I'd prefer to do a few shifts than borrow money."

"Jeeze, you're a stubborn bastard, Toby. Why don't you let someone help you out every now and then? Your mum was the same. She'd always insist I take her money, and I did to make her feel comfortable. But I left it on the top of the counter next to the front door."

"Did she ever say anything about it?"

"Yeah. She went crook a few times. But I couldn't take it from her. You guys were struggling enough."

"I guess it sort of runs in the family. Bill was the same. He was so stubborn when he wanted to be."

"Yep, you can say that again. And so is Tristan."

"Tristan? Who's Tristan?"

He looks over at me, lets out a sigh, then gives a warm smile. "Tristan is Bill's boy."

In the beats of silence that follow, I swallow loudly. I look at him open-mouthed.

"Tristan is your nephew, Toby." He grins. "That's why I came here today, to let Bill know he has a son."

I close my mouth.

"And I would like for you to come by and meet him."

I don't respond. My brain can't process any other thoughts. "Bill has a boy."

"Yes."

"I have a nephew."

"Yes." Picker laughs.

When my mind relaxes, I feel the happiness explode out of me with the thought of still having a part of Bill here with me. "What's he like?"

"He's definitely Bill's boy. He's a little rascal like his father. Spit-image of him."

The tears fill my eyes.

"So, shall I tell the wife to expect you for dinner?"

"Yes, I would like that."

"Good. I'll see you then." He stands and downs the last of his ale, plonks his hat back on his head, and climbs onto his horse.

I keep watch as he rides down the driveway.

By the time I've weeded the long grass from my mother's grave, it's well after five in the afternoon, and I start the short hike over to Picker's farm. I will admit meeting Tristan makes me feel a little nervous, but excited at the same time.

Taking my time wandering down the long driveway, I stare up at the long farmhouse. It's tough being here without Bill. We practically grew up here. It's a place, along with our own home, where we felt comfortable being ourselves. As always, the house is impeccably neat. Picker's wife, Gabrielle, is busy sweeping the front porch. I am absently looking at her when, out the corner of my eye, I catch sight of a snowy-haired boy racing across the yard. I slow for a minute and allow my eyes to follow him. I watch him creep on tippy toes down along the garden path towards the ginger cat relaxing near the stables. I smile as he stands entirely still as if con-templating his next move. Suddenly, the boy pounces. Tail aloft, the cat scurries ahead. The little boy falls to the ground empty handed. Dust clouds erupt, temporarily obscuring the boy. He coughs and then stands and marches off, stalking the cat all over again.

There is something so magical standing there watching this little boy continue on with his game. Even though I haven't met him yet, he somehow seems so familiar.

After his fifth attempt, he stands, dusts off his clothes, and turns, leaving the cat behind him. It's only a matter of seconds before he catches sight of me standing there. He stops and gawks at me. I can't help but stare back. The resemblance to Bill is uncanny.

"Well, hello there, Mister," he yells out, crossing the yard. "What's your name?" He stops and looks up at me with those recognisable blue eyes.

"My name is Toby."

"Are you here to visit my poppy?"

"Yes, I am. Your poppy invited me over for dinner."

I glance up. Gabrielle smiles and gives me a wave. I wave back.

"Did you know my dad's a soldier? His away fighting in the war." He scratches the end of his dusty nose. "My poppy says he's very brave."

"Yes, I know he's a soldier, and I also think he's brave." My eyes tear up.

"So, you know him then?"

"Yes, I know your daddy. Quite well in fact." As I talk, my heart swells with so much love for this little boy I've only just met. My eyes continue to absorb him. He has the same cowlick at the front of his forehead as the one Bill always complained about. He has dimples that match his father's. They lie dormant within his cheeks and appear only when his face breaks into a smile. "You look like your dad."

"That's what my mum says." He tosses a look back over his shoulder. "Do you see that cat over there?"

"Yes," I say, lifting my eyes.

He turns his face back. "Do you think you could help me catch that cat?"

"Why do you want to catch the cat?"

"There's a rat in the shed." Suddenly his eyes widen. "Maybe we can catch the rat instead?"

"No!" I laugh out loud. "I think the cat will do."

"Okay, then, Mister. Let's go get the cat." He slips his tiny hand into mine, and I follow.

19

After a week of getting to know Tristan, I decide I can no longer put off the much-needed repairs to the house. With the local timber yard closed, I need to make the two-hour hike to the nearest town.

I wake up early and collect Picker's truck to make the trip.

When I arrive at the town, the traffic is almost at a standstill. I jolt the truck into first gear and drive slowly down the busy main street. A sea of people of all ages crowds the dual carriageway as they shift between old wooden shops. I've been here before, but I can't recall it being this busy, although I was only a boy at the time. My mother sold one of her patchwork quilts to purchase three tickets so Bill and I could experience a ride on a train for the first time. I've never forgotten that beautiful memory—sitting there, watching the countryside race by and listening to the sound of the engine. It was every little boy's dream.

It takes a good twenty minutes for me to find a parking space. I open the truck door, step out into the warm, humid air and give my back a good stretch.

I slide my hand down into my pocket and drag out a long list of supplies. I trace my finger down over every word, searing each item into my memory.

As I roam the streets, no one pays attention to me. I can't recollect the last time that happened—no one staring, no one judging me with their prejudiced eyes. Taking my time, I glance into every shopfront window. I check out the colourful array of arts and crafts, the newest fashionable fabrics, the hats and fedoras, even the bright lolly display. Nothing is off limits.

It is then, as I walk around the corner, that my heart skips a beat. A lump forms in the back of my throat as my eyes consume every inch of her. She is no longer that tall, lanky girl I remember, but a beautiful young woman. Her closeness makes my breath stall in my lungs. I half wonder if it's all a dream, and it's now time to wake up.

She looks so beautiful in her red fitted dress and her long white gloves. She has her hair pinned up, exposing her long, thin neck. She seems so happy as she stands there chatting with two other people. I shift on my feet as the old insecurities, from years ago, slowly leak in. What if she never wants to see me again because of what happened? I think about taking off, but for some reason, my body won't shift. My legs begin to shake in a way I cannot control.

She finishes her conversation, turns, and walks along the footpath. The minute her eyes fall on me, she does a double take and stops.

For the longest time, we stand there, staring at each other. I pull my hands out of my pockets. Now I'm unsure what to do with them. Around me, I hear the loud noise of car engines as the traffic passes. A person yells out from somewhere in the street. As I stand utterly still, my mind shifts in different directions. What should I do? Do I leave, or will I wait and let her go first? But the moment she gives me a most brilliant smile, I relax.

Within seconds, she's rushing over. Nervously, I scratch the stubble on the base of my chin as I watch her stride break into a run. I'm still shaking as she flings her arms up around my neck. And then, as if it's the most familiar thing to do, I wrap my arms around her and pull her in close.

"Oh, Toby!" she whispers, nuzzling the side of her face into my neck. "I've missed you so much!"

I close my eyes and just hold her, breathing in her familiar scent. Just the mere touch of her makes me realise how much I've craved her over the years. The love stirs in me, the same way it did when I was seventeen.

As our embrace lingers, people shift around us.

"I can't believe it's you!" She leans back and stares up at me with those green eyes, the ones I remember from a lifetime ago. "For a moment there I thought my eyes were playing tricks on me. I couldn't believe it was you standing there." She laughs, lifts her gloved hands, and cups the sides of my face. "What are you doing here?" Her eyes roam over my face. No doubt she's noticing the changes in me, the same way I am seeing them in her.

"The mill at home is closed, so I'm here to get some timber." My eyes never leave her face. "But, gosh, it's good to see you, Hildy." I can't stop smiling.

"It's so wonderful to see you too, Toby." She smiles, drops her arms, and deposits her hands into mine. "Oh, please tell me you have time to stay and catch up. I have so much to tell you. And I would really love to hear about what you've been up to."

"Yeah, of course I can stay." Looking up, I see her sister, Beatrice, standing only a few feet behind Hildy, watching us with critical eyes.

Hildy turns in the direction of my gaze. The moment she spots Beatrice standing there, she snatches her hands away as if they've been burnt. Her head switches back and forth as her eyes flick between Beatrice and me.

A few seconds later, she drops her face, and I watch her swallow. "Please forgive me, Toby." She whispers. When she peers back up, her expression has changed, her smile has dissolved, her whole body is stiff. She steps back a few paces. "It's been a real pleasure seeing you again." The mist appears in her eyes. "But I really must be going."

I reach out and take hold of her arm before she departs. "Hildy, please don't do this."

She hesitates but keeps her head down. "I have to go, Toby. I thought by now you would realise that I don't want to be seen with the likes of you. Leave me alone." She yanks her arm free from my grip.

I stay planted on the spot and watch her leave. Not once does she bother to look back at me. And just like that, the current comes in and washes her away all over again. I know those words were for Beatrice's benefit, but it still didn't stop them from stinging. When I lose sight of her in among the crowd, my eyes veer to Beatrice who is still standing a few feet away from me. "Are you happy now?" I ask her.

A catlike smile stretches across her lips. "Yes, in fact, I am, thank you." She swings her shoulders around and chases after Hildy.

In all the times I've fantasied about seeing her again, never once did it end like this. People stare at me as I pace between the road and the baker's shop. Why did she let Beatrice dictate her actions? That's not like Hildy. She never cared what her sister thought before.

What to do. The ideas come hard and fast and flash through my mind. Ten minutes later, I'm racing through the streets, searching through the crowd for her red dress. I need to see her again. I have to tell her that I can't cope without her, that life is full of uncertainties, but I'm confident of one thing— I've never stopped loving her.

After checking every alleyway, every shop, I stop on the corner and wait. Sweat trickles down the centre of my back, leaving behind a path of moisture that drenches my shirt. With one hand shoved into my pocket, I stand there. Glancing around, I continue to search.

The hours pass as the sun moves across the sky, and still my search drags on.

With time rapidly running out, I take out my shopping list, and with what little money I have from two work shifts, I charge around the town to gather supplies.

With the truck loaded up and my stomach growling impatiently, I survey the area one last time. Nothing.

As I slide in behind the steering wheel, the intensity of seeing her hits me, and tears surge. I let out a long sigh and close my eyes. If only I'd known she was here all along. I could have come to her sooner. I open my eyes and give one last look down the road before starting the vehicle. If I want answers, then I will have to find her again, but first I need to step back and let everything settle in my mind.

The rest of the drive is a bit of a blur. All I remember is shutting off the engine and staring out through the windscreen at the house. I sit there in the truck for a long time.

The image of Hildy stays with me all through the night.

20

The nightmares return that night. However, they are a little different. We are no longer those teenage kids but the adults we are right now. The end is the same though. I cannot protect her. Either way, those dreams are still unbearable.

So, instead of lying there torturing myself, I get up. I have to occupy my mind.

After a quick bite, I grab a hammer and work under the faint glow of the front porch light. I work solidly, ripping up the front steps, replacing the old rotten boards with the new. I press my body hard. I have to destroy those awful dreams. But no matter how hard I seek to push myself, Hildy is all I think about. I can't make sense of why she didn't let me know she was only two hours away. All these years I've been so lost without her. Why couldn't she have got in touch with me? Was Bill right? Was she not as happy to see me as I wanted to believe?

When the steps are complete, I straighten my stiff back and stare out into the new morning light into the silence until I hear a kookaburra laugh.

A few minutes after that, I make my way across the front yard and into the shed. I grab the ladder and arm myself with a few wooden planks. I set the ladder and climb my way up.

The hours pass, and with the heat of the day, my body soon grows tired. Grabbing a well-earned break, I sit down on the newly set beams, letting my legs dangle freely down over the side of the shed. The sun floods its warmth on my back as I soak up the view. Never have I seen a picture as beautiful as this. I notice a lady in yellow wandering down the road. She must have taken a wrong turn up at Chipper's Lane because, out here, she looks a little out of place in her fancy dress and matching sunhat. I shift my attention across to Picker's farm where three black horses are bolting off across the paddock. Each free-spirited mare sprays her tail high in the air as they move together as one. I watch them for a while longer. It is only then that I notice that the woman in the yellow dress has strayed into my driveway. I silently curse myself for not replacing the hinges. She must have seen me up on the roof, and now she's coming in to ask for directions.

She stops and just stands in the driveway for a moment peering down at the house. Then, after a while, she continues on. I keep watching her until she lifts her head. Then, as if emerging out of a dream, one by one, her features come into view. My mouth is dry. My eyes become misty. My heart races. I sit there stock-still as she walks over to the house and stops at the bottom step.

By the time I'm back down the ladder and racing across the yard, Hildy's already at the front door. As I step forward, my eyes soak up every inch of her—her perfect hourglass figure, the loose curls peeking out from under her hat. She is so unaware of her beauty.

Just as her knuckles tap against the door, I move up onto the first step. "Hello, Hildy."

She pivots to the sound of my voice. After a long searching look, she drops her gaze down to her white-gloved hands. "I'm sorry. I know it's rude to just show up uninvited but ..." She releases a long breath and swallows before looking back up. "Well, I couldn't stand to leave things the way I did yesterday." She looks away. "The things I said ... Toby, I only said them because ..." She breathes in and fidgets with the fingers of her gloves. "I'm sorry. I shouldn't have come back here to bother you." She rushes forward, down the first step and then the next.

My reflexes immediately snap in. I don't want her to leave. I step into her path. She pauses on the step above me, our eyes level.

Breathing hard, Hildy looks down, concentrating on my sweaty, crumpled shirt.

"Don't go, Hildy. Please stay." My heart thumps painfully in my chest as I wait for her reply.

Her eyes rise and stop at my face. "Okay," she whispers, nodding slightly.

"Good." Smiling, I move up onto the step beside her and look out over the countryside.

For the longest time, we stand there, neither one of us uttering a single word. There's something so guarded about her today. She seems different to the joyful person I saw yesterday. I shuffle from foot to foot and wonder if she's thought about me over the years as I have of her.

Leaning back, I capture her image out the corner of my eye. Has too much time passed between us? Is that why, now, this all feels so awkward? The concept alone makes me a little shaky on my feet. With all these unanswered questions forming in my head, it takes me a moment to realise Hildy is speaking.

"It's so beautiful out here. It's just as I remembered." Her eyes seek mine, and she smiles. "I can't believe I'm standing here." She swings her face away. I watch her breathe.

As we stand there, a part of me wants to take her hand in mine, to pull her into me and tell her all the things I need to say. But I don't. The uncomfortable silence between us continues. Finally, after what seems like forever, my brain produces a sentence.

"You must be thirsty?"

"Yes," she says with a nod.

"Is lemonade okay?"

"Yes, thank you." Hildy turns her head and stares at me. "You make lemonade now?"

"No, Mrs. Picker made it. Would you like to come in?"

"I might stay out here if that's okay."

"Yes, of course." I move up to the next step. "Come take a seat." I gesture with my hand over to the wooden chairs.

She turns and climbs back up the stairs.

I pause as she cuts across in front of me before I make my way over to the door. Pulling open the screen, I glance back over my shoulder and watch Hildy take off her hat and then her long, white gloves. "Hildy," I say.

She twists her head.

"I'm happy you came to visit today."

When I return minutes later, I pause at the doorway and look out through the screen. Hildy is sitting there motionless in the chair staring out over the land. Her hair is luminous in the sunshine. I push open the door. When I'm at her side, she takes one of the tall glasses from my hand. I take a sip of lemonade as I sit in the seat next to her. "I was up on the shed putting on a new roof when I saw you walking down the road." I pause to wipe my sweaty hands on my pants. "I didn't know it was you until you got close."

"You were up there?" She looks towards the shed. "I didn't even see you."

"How did you get here?"

Shaking her head, she takes in a long breath and lets it out. "Believe it or not, I caught the train." She takes a sip and rests the glass against her bottom lip.

"What?"

"I know. Right." She laughs. "It's so crazy. Something just came over me. I heard the train, knew it was coming this way, and I got on."

"Just like that?"

"Yes. Although ..." She frowns, shifting her gaze down to her lap. "I really didn't think it through because there isn't a train back for another two days. I have no clothes or even a place to stay for that matter. It was silly of me to do that."

"Well, that's easy. You can stay here. Problem fixed."

She lifts her head. "Oh, no, I wouldn't want to intrude. I shall organise someplace back in town."

"Hildy, it's not a problem, and besides, it will be good to hear what you've been up to all these years."

"But what about the others? I wouldn't want to intrude on them."

"There are no others." I lean back in the chair. "I'm the only one left here now."

Her eyes and mouth are round with shock. Slowly her hand comes up over her mouth. "Oh, Toby, I'm so sorry. I had no idea. I didn't know."

"I know you didn't."

We remain silent.

"Here, let me grab you another drink, and I will explain it all. Then it will be your turn."

As the sun passes over the sky, I tell Hildy all about my mother's death and the circumstances of her burial that contributed to Bill's addiction. Throughout the story, I catch her dabbing her lace handkerchief at the edges of her eyes. I then tell her how Bill defeated his demons and how he disappeared from my side. Her tears fall like rain. I want to go to her and comfort her, but I'm afraid it would scare her away. Instead, I speak of Tristan and tell her the story of the rat.

She laughs out loud. "Oh, I wish I could meet him, Toby. He sounds just like Bill."

"Yeah, he's identical."

She lets out a long breath. "Okay, well I suppose it's my turn now." She peers down and traces her finger around the rim of her glass. "Gosh, where do I start? I suppose I'll begin with the night you and Bill took me home. No need to tell you how that went."

"Yes. It didn't go well for any of us." I take a sip of my drink.

"After the two of you left, my mother announced that, if I had anything to do with you or Bill or even your mother, then she would call the authorities to have you both arrested for what happened to me." She shifts in the chair.

"Your mother knew it wasn't us who harmed you, didn't she?"

"Yes. I made sure of that, but she didn't care. It was her way of pointing out that, if I had anything to do with either one of you, there would be consequences." She rests the glass down in her lap. "Apparently, my parents had bought a new house a few months previously, but they'd said nothing about it to Beatrice or me. We moved in the middle of the night. Honestly, I'm sure they did it so I couldn't let you or Bill know that I was going." She keeps her eyes fixed on her glass. "I've wanted to come back so many times over the years to tell you I was okay and where I was. I've written so many letters. It's just ..." She swallows. "Well, I could never post them. I was worried my parents would discover that I'd written to you and then follow through with the threat." She lifts her head and stares into my face, her eyes searching as if seeking forgiveness for all the pain she has caused me over the years. "I'd never be able to forgive myself if that were to happen. I'm so sorry, Toby, for everything." She lifts her hand and swipes a finger in under her eye. "I didn't mean to hurt you. I just didn't know what else to do. I'm sorry."

As I sit there listening to her story, I think back to that night. I can picture in my head her parents standing over her, making those offensive threats. I feel sick at the thought of it. It all makes sense—the way she disappeared, why she never reached out to me, even yesterday, the way Beatrice controlled her actions.

"It's fine, Hildy." I shake my head and give a flicker of a smile. "I did constantly wonder where you were and if you were all right. But I understand why you thought you couldn't let me know."

She gazes steadily at me before turning her face back to the view.

I digest her words for several minutes, gazing up as a flock of white cockatoos fly overhead. "So ... tell me more. What else has been happening?" I ask.

She takes a deep breath, like someone who is about to make a formal speech. "W-well, as it turns out, my parents are a real hit at our new place." She pushes her hair off her face. "It does help to be one of the richest families in town." She leans in and gently taps my arm, a hint of the old Hildy shines through.

"And as you know, money is the only thing that matters in this world ... apparently."

I laugh out loud.

"Bea got married last year to some jerk my parents chose for her. You know what it's like—someone who fits into the social ladder." She shifts her legs out in front, tugging her dress down over her knees. "Bea's not happy. I can clearly see that. She didn't want to marry him, but my father talked her round."

I take a long sip of lemonade before I find the courage to ask. "And what about you, Hildy? Have they chosen someone for you?" I shift in my chair, breathing out a deep sigh. My heart thumps loudly in my chest.

"Oh, they've tried, I'll give them that." She looks down and swirls the remaining lemonade around in the glass. "They've chosen a few plausible husbands, you could say." She squints at something on the far horizon. "But if I'm to be blunt, every one of them annoyed me. All they did was boast about what they want, or how much wealth their parents had. I've told my parents so often I'm not interested in any of them."

"And what did they say to that?"

"They didn't care. They simply said I was immature, and it was time for me to be married. So, I decided I had to deal with the problem myself."

"Why? What do you mean?"

She raises her eyebrows and giggles. "I had to make those suitors run for the hills. Every time my parents left me alone with any of them, I would be obnoxious. I mean detestable! I would talk over the top of them whenever they spoke. If they made a comment about anything, then I would tell them they were wrong and make up my own story about it. I was shocking. Sometimes it worked, and on those rare occasions it didn't, I'd mention I could hear voices in my head.

"Oh, tell me you didn't." I laugh out loud.

"Yes, I did." She tosses her head back and gives a hearty chuckle. It's a sound I haven't heard for so long, I can't help but smile. "And to make it more convincing one time, I had to have a debate with myself."

"So, did it work?"

"Oh, yes! He rushed right out of the room."

The laughter that follows is so familiar. It's a flashback to the way we used to be together. I look at her steadily, taking in the tiny creases at the edges of her eyes as she smiles. She seems more at ease now. All the conflicting emotions I saw an hour ago are long gone.

"Oh gosh," Hildy adds, wiping the tears from her cheeks. "I haven't laughed like this since …" She frowns and shakes her head. "I can't remember the last time."

"Yeah, I know exactly what you mean."

Perhaps it's the pleasure of sitting out there with a person who once knew everything about me, or maybe it's that I have someone to talk to, but to have her here at my side again makes me feel whole. She feels like home. Something inside me whispers that day that, even though the past has been written by others, it is now up to me to create my future by telling her how I still feel.

21

If anyone has seen us that day, they would think we looked comfortable sitting there in the peaceful silence, sipping our lemonades, looking out across the land. But, in truth, I am as nervous as hell. I could always express my love to her, so why am I so worried?

When it comes to around five in the afternoon, I realise I haven't had anything to eat since early this morning. And I can only presume it would be the same for Hildy. I turn to her. "Are you hungry?"

"Yes, I believe I am," she says, as though she'd only just realised it.

"Come on then, let's go get something to eat." I stand and hold my palm out to her.

She slides her hand into mine as she gets up.

As Hildy steps into the house, I stay over near the door and watch her as she remembers the front room. Her green eyes are intent, her face is serious as she glances at the many photographs. Her long hair tumbles down over her back in a wave of curls. I want to stroke my hand through it, to feel the softness once again.

Moving in behind the old lounge, Hildy traces her fingers across the colourful patchwork quilt. "I remember this. I can't believe your mother finished it. We were only halfway through if I remember rightly. She did a great job of it." Hildy seems crushed by the memories.

Stepping into the middle of the room, I desperately want to touch her, as if somehow that might magically wipe away all the time that has passed between us and blot out all that's happened and take us back to be those joyous, carefree kids we once were.

"Your mother was beautiful. So caring." The sadness shows through. "I could see how much love she had for you and Bill. It radiated out of her."

I move closer to her.

"This might sound silly, Toby, but on those days when I waited for you to come home when I was sewing in the kitchen with your mother, well ... I kind of pretended she was my mother too." She squeezes her eyes shut.

I touch her arm.

Her eyes snap open. She looks up at me, the tears fill her eyes.

"Hildy you meant a great deal to her too. And I am sure she would have been thrilled to know you thought of her that way." I smile. "On her good days, she would always ask after you."

"Really?" She forces a lopsided smile. "Or are you just telling me that to make me feel better?"

"It's the truth. I promise. On those days when Bill and I came home from work, she would have the needle already threaded for you."

"And when I didn't show up, what did you say then?"

"Bill told her you must have been held up in town and you'd get here when you could."

She peers back to the quilt, and tears surge. She's silent for the moment as if lost somewhere in all the painful reminders. "I've made a mess of everything, haven't I?"

I shake my head. "She was fine, Hildy." I grab hold of her fingers. With my thumb, I lightly stroke the back of her hand. "I promise you that, on those days she knew you would get here when you were able to, Bill and I made sure she understood. It didn't upset her. She said she would complete another square and let you do the next one tomorrow."

"Thank you. I would hate to think that I hurt her as well." A tear escapes. She quickly swipes it away. "Oh, will you look at me. I'm so silly."

"It's not silly, Hildy." I hold a smile. "Now let's not think about that. Let's get something to eat."

"Okay." She looks at me and nods.

Together we walk through to the kitchen. Within minutes, I've got the pan sizzling away on the stove. As I move across to the cupboard and grab two cups, Hildy's eyes are watching me.

"Can I help with anything?" Her hands lift and run back through her hair, pushing the long curls behind her shoulders. "Do you want me to make the tea?"

"Yeah, if you like. Or you can do the eggs." I point to the pan on the stove. "Whichever. It's up to you."

She turns from me and looks to the stove. "The eggs. I'll do the eggs. You make the tea."

I grab hold of the kettle. Behind me, Hildy lets out a spontaneous laugh. "What?" I ask.

"I just remembered that day when Bill cooked us lunch." She giggles. "Oh, please tell me you remember that?"

"Yeah, I do." I smile, remembering the way it had been with the three of us. "How could I ever forget that? It was the worst thing I ever tasted."

"I know. Right?" She pauses. "Do you recall it being so bad that Bill couldn't even eat it?" She holds a hand across her stomach and laughs out loud again. "And especially when he made the big announcement that it was the best thing he'd ever cooked."

I pause, kettle in hand, enjoying her laughter.

"And remember how cocky he was? How he boasted that he may have to take on the cooking duties? And then, that look on his face when he ate it. Oh, I will never forget that." Her laughter rolls around the room. "You know I always liked Bill. Even that first day when I met him here in the kitchen, I liked him. When I was down the hallway, I could pick up everything he was saying. I found it quite entertaining that he had such a strong opinion of me." She doesn't move for a moment. "I bet you miss him."

"Yeah, I do. I think of him every day. Every little thing triggers a memory."

There is absolute silence as we stand there eyeing each other.

Hildy's the first to speak. "Bill and I used to sit together in the living room while you were cooking your mother's meal and just talk."

"What did you talk about?"

"I don't know." She shrugs. "Just different things. Like what people were saying about your mother. You know, the usual stuff. Under all that hardness and strength he presented to the world, I saw a different side of him. He let his shield down, and I saw the helplessness, the struggle." She bites down on her bottom lip and turns back to the stove. "He was always kind to me. Many times I've thought of him over the years."

"Yeah, well, I know for a fact he really cared about you. He told me so."

Her mouth quivers slightly, as a deep pain enters her eyes.

At that point, I couldn't mention the truth. How could I? How could I tell her he had fallen in love with her, and he'd been just as broken without her as I was? I prefer her to look back on their beautiful relationship with sincerity, joy, and warmth instead of doubting all his motives. I change the subject. "Do you remember the first day down at the river with the mud?"

She laughs under her breath. "Yes."

"Later that night Bill wanted to know if you had any sisters."

"Really?" she answers over her shoulder. "And what did you say to him?"

"I told him that you did, but she was different to you."

"And what did he say to that?"

"He said nothing."

"No?"

"Nope. Because he understood what I meant."

"Oh."

As we eat, the conversation comes out naturally. Hildy's lips curl just as they used to when she's about to say something funny. Her eyes shut when she giggles. I never imagined I could fall in love all over again with the person who already owned my heart, but I did.

Sitting there listening to her, I lose all aspect of time. It's not until I see the afternoon sun spearing in through the small-framed window that I realise most of the day has gone.

"Come on." I get up from my chair and take hold of her hand. "We have to hurry, or we're going to miss it."

Her face lifts after the words register. Then she's quickly on her feet.

We stumble out onto the verandah. The noise of the back door slamming intrudes into the silence. Having Hildy next to me, showing her the sunset once again, makes me feel as if our history is catching up with us.

Outside, nothing can compare with the beauty of the setting sun. All the merging oranges and pinks splash together across the sky until the intensity and power of the last glimmer of light are finally surrendered to the darkness.

Hildy lets go of my hand and sits in one of the rockers, her eyes staying locked on the far horizon. "I can't believe you still do this. After all these years, Toby, you haven't changed at all. You still honour and respect everything the world has to offer. I've never met anyone like you. And I don't suppose I ever will." She turns to me, her face is aglow. "And, yes, before you ask, it's a good thing."

"Well, I do it to honour my mother and my brother."

"It's wonderful of you." She turns her attention back to the horizon. "Your mother was right. It really is like heaven."

We quiet our minds and sit comfortably watching the kaleidoscope of colour dissipate into the shadows. As the night deepens, I find my eyes sneaking back over to glance at Hildy. There's an ache flowing through me as I watch the moonlight stream down over her face. I've loved her from the moment I first saw her. Often, over the years, Picker has told me that the pain of losing someone dulls with time, but it has never been like that for me. Long ago, she carved herself into my soul, and my love for her will never change. This would be my life now, sitting here next to her if only that monster had not appeared. How will I ever survive if she walks out of my life again? I have to tell Hildy how I feel before it's too late.

I turn my head, and whatever I'm about to say is lost when she blinks, and a silent teardrop slides down over her cheek. Now is not the right time to tell her.

As the cool night air drifts in, I consider heading back inside into the warmth. I cut a look across to Hildy, simply to discover her eyes are closed. Her only movement is the slight rise and fall of her chest. She looks so peaceful sitting there. I don't want to disturb her.

I get up from the chair and move inside. It's only a matter of minutes before I'm back with a patchwork quilt in each hand. I drop one down into my rocker and then lean forward and set the quilt down over Hildy, tenderly tucking the edges in under her chin and around her shoulders. For the longest time, my eyes devour her face, taking in those familiar lips. The faint scar embedded on her top lip is a tormenting reminder of that horrible day. I take in her perfectly shaped cheekbones, her smooth silky skin. Out here, she is free and untamed, not bounded by the social etiquette standards thrust upon her every day. I lift my hand, longing with all my being to reach out and touch her beautiful face, to feel the tenderness in my hand once more. But at the last second, I refrain from doing so as I do not want to wake her. I will have to continue torturing myself watching her without being able to touch.

I turn away, take my seat next to her, and pull the quilt in under my chin. Somewhere out in the night an owl hoots.

22

The next morning at daybreak I give in to the wakefulness. I open my eyes as the land around me wakes in its own natural rhythm. Drawing the quilt in under my chin, I forget for the moment as to why I am out here. Then I come to and glance sideways. Hildy is still sleeping. As I sit there, I think about how easy it was back when we were young when I would pull her in close to me and kiss her cheek, reach out and take her hand. What we had in our youth had been so unique. It was the kind of magic people yearned for. Back then, I was saturated with a sense that we could do anything together, be anything we wanted to be. It felt as if we were starting out our life together. When did it all get so complicated that I now struggle to tell her how I feel?

Pushing the thoughts from my head, I get up from the chair and make my way inside.

I quickly prepare a fire and warm the stove. By the time I've stacked a dozen or so pancakes down onto the plate, I become aware of Hildy standing in the doorway with the quilt wrapped in tightly around her shoulders.

Would anyone find her more beautiful than I do at this exact moment? The way her unruly hair twists down around her shoulders. I just stare at her. It is only when I hear the kettle spluttering away on the stove that I draw back into the moment. I rush across the room and lift the kettle from off the hotplate.

"Hey. I didn't wake you, did I?" I turn back to her.

"No."

"Are you hungry?"

Hildy's eyes flicker to the plate of pancakes on the table and then back at me. "That looks good. But first, let me freshen up a bit," she says, lifting her hand up in an attempt to fix her wild mane. "I must look like a fright."

"Of course. While you do that, I'll get the coffees." I turn around but stop halfway. "And, Hildy, you look as beautiful as ever." As our eyes linger for a second, she flushes and then drops her head. Just as she turns away, I catch a smile spreading over her mouth.

Soon after I've brewed the coffee and set our places at the table, the bathroom door creaks open. Within seconds, Hildy glides into the kitchen.

"I hope you don't mind, but I grabbed one of your mum's dresses from the cupboard."

"Yes, that's fine." I glance up. It was like turning back the clock. The girl from my youth is standing right in front of me, her long wild wet hair hanging down around her shoulders, framing her face. "Just grab whatever you need."

"I didn't think you'd mind. I need to have my dress fresh for the trip back tomorrow."

As she approaches, I shove a cup of coffee into her hand. "Thank you." She wraps both hands around the mug, takes a sip, and then slides down into a seat at the dinner table.

"Pancakes. I can't recall the last time I had pancakes." She peers up and smiles.

Sipping my coffee, I watch her plate up and then add a generous splash of golden syrup. She looks at me then.

"Aren't you having any?"

"I will in a minute." I take a sip of coffee.

"Toby, may I ask you something?" She keeps her eyes down on the plate in front.

"Sure. What is it?" I shift in the chair, setting my cup down on the table. "You can ask me anything."

She glances up, and I see the softness in her eyes. "Do you ever think about ...?" She pauses for a while as she collects her thoughts. "What I mean is ... do you ever wish things could have worked out differently from the way they did?

"Of course I do."

"What I mean is ..." She takes in a deep breath and lets it out with a sigh.

"If you're wondering if I have thought about you over the years, the answer to that question is yes, every single day." I pull out a chair from under the table and sit down next to her. "Every day I wondered where you were. If you were all right. If you were happy. Hildy, you were all I ever thought about. You want me to be honest? I felt so broken without you here."

I half expect her to say something, to add anything about the way she feels, but she doesn't. She merely swallows and reaches for her cup and takes a sip. I suddenly realise I've said too much.

The kitchen falls silent. The only interruption is the ticking sound of the clock.

I pick up a fork and serve up a few pancakes.

"Toby, when we finish breakfast, could you take me back to the river?"

I hesitate. "Can I ask why?" Keeping my eyes down on my plate, I spear a piece of pancake with my fork.

"Despite what happened there, I still have fond memories of that place." Hildy stops eating. "It's where I saw the real you that first day."

I look up.

A gentle smile graces her lips. "It's where I got to know Bill and Sam. It's where you taught me to skim stones. I need those memories to stay with me."

I give her a quick smile and then pop a piece of pancake into my mouth.

"Please say you will take me there so I can see it again."

Feelings of guilt rush to the surface, and for the moment I am not exactly sure how to answer, so instead, I offer a weak smile and nod.

With breakfast out of the way, Hildy stands and collects the dirty plates and takes them across to the sink.

"So, are you ready to go now? Or do you have a few things you have to do first?" She spins around and leans her hip against the sink.

"Hildy, there's something I need to confess." I take a moment to compose myself. "I haven't been back to the river."

"Since when?"

The seconds seem to pass like minutes as I sit there. "Since that day."

"Are you serious?"

"Yes." I lift my face.

She glides across the room, sits down in the chair opposite, and coils her fingers around my hand. "The memory of that day still haunts you."

I nod my head slowly before answering. "That's why I can't understand why you want to go back there."

"Oh, Toby, there are days when that memory sits heavy in me too. I understand that. But I want to go back there so I can feel like my old self again. This was the one place where I could honestly be myself. I didn't have to worry about someone reporting back to my parents about what I had done, or Bea dobbing on any little thing. We were just kids, Toby, but I still carry the memory of this place everywhere I go. It means more to me than you will ever know. You, your brother, your mother, the wildflowers, and the river. Every bit of it gave me a sense of belonging. I've never belonged anywhere. That's why I need to go back. Because I'm losing all those special, wonderful memories and how I felt being there. I need to feel that again." She squeezes my hand. "Plus, I do remember you saying that the river was your favourite place. After that first day, it also became mine too." She gives me a smile and blinks away a tear. "That man took our innocence away that day. And we are both scarred forever. I understand if you can't go back, but don't you think he has taken enough from us? It's now your choice to determine if you let him take all the good away from you as well."

Sitting there, looking at her, I realise she's right. I have allowed him to control that part of my life. After everything she has been through, after she survived it all on her own, I come to realise she is the strongest person I have ever known. "How did you get so wise?"

She lets go of my hand. "I've always been wise. It's just taken you a little time to figure that out. But when I think about it, I wasn't wise enough to bring a change of clothes with me, now was I?" She grins for a second and then gets up from the table.

I drink down the last of my coffee, and before I can change my mind, I stand. "Okay. Let's go."

In less than five minutes, we are weaving our way through the tall grass. In some odd way, it feels as if we've stepped through a wormhole that's hurled us back to our youth. The only difference is that our roles are reversed; this time Hildy holds my hand, leading the way.

Above us, the sky is crammed with dark bloated clouds. Around me, I absorb every sound. Each tuft of grass bends and rustles with the wind, and the chorus of birdsong is like music to the soul.

I look ahead, watching Hildy's hair whip around in the breeze. I take in the delicate sway of her body as it moves in the loose-fitting dress.

Suddenly, hundreds of birds explode out from the tall grass, sprinting high into the sky. As we lift our faces to watch, I am lost in a momentary conjuration of my childhood. How I would love to relive those brilliant days, bolting through the grass chasing Bill, making as much noise as possible, just to check out those painted birds soaring across the sky.

We roam the full length of the field, and as soon as the wildflowers come into view, Hildy releases my hand. Then she's off, tearing her way through the valley, arms raised out to her sides. The sight of her rekindles memories that I have long forgotten. It's as if nothing has changed between us, and I am that seventeen-year-old boy again, staring at my crush.

Slipping my hands into my pockets, I relax and enjoy this rare, wonderful moment. I'd forgotten how beautiful this place could be. It feels as if I am visiting an old friend. I close my eyes, allowing all the calm to soak in. I want to go back to that innocent kid, to a time when everything seemed right in the world. A time before the war. Before the attack on Hildy. That way I can be prepared and know exactly how to keep her safe. I open my eyes.

Hildy stops and checks back over her shoulder for me. When our eyes meet, a smile spreads across her face. Her happiness is so infectious that it passes right through me. I beam my own grin back at her.

"Oh, they're just as I remembered!" She swings around and starts walking back to me, her fingers tracing over the velvety petals. "But I don't recall there being so many butterflies."

As she drifts towards me, I note that time has not changed her. She is still that free-spirited, fun-loving girl. After all the years of loss and pain I have suffered, she is the only person who is able to make me feel like my old self again.

She pauses less than twenty yards short of me. "Are you coming or what?"

I nod and go forward. For the longest time, Hildy's eyes watch me as I close the gap. The silence stretches. I am now aware of her heavy breathing, which is becoming deeper and stronger with every repetition. Something is changing between us. I can feel it.

The minute I step in close to her, my heart thumps against the wall of my chest. Peering down into her green eyes, I yearn to touch her, to kiss her, to feel her hair in my hands—anything that will let me feel closer to her. My faltering logic reminds me I need to do something to keep her here.

Unexpectedly, Hildy turns her head away, ruining the moment. I silently curse myself for not leaning forward to taste those warm lips.

I glance down to the wildflowers brushing against my legs. Kneeling, I snap a stem clean off in my fingers. How could something so delicate, so fragile, and yet so beautiful survive untouched all these years in all the chaos? I stand and look at the girl who stands opposite. And, as I had done before, in what seems like a lifetime ago, I gift her the wildflower.

She smiles, looks down at the flower, studies it, and then pulls it in under her nose, inhaling the sweet perfume.

The wind picks up and sweeps around us. I grab Hildy's hand, and we walk together through the valley, frequently stopping to admire the view. With each passing stride, the river's pull feels stronger as if, in some abnormal way, it's calling out to me the way it did when I was a boy.

When we step up onto the rise and look out over the water, we abruptly stop. The mere sight of the place sends snatches of information into my mind—the memory I desperately wanted to forget. A shudder goes through me as every detail of that horrible day plays back through my mind—his wolflike eyes, the pain on the back of my neck. I'm back there again watching Hildy's legs collapse underneath her.

Hildy is shaking so hard, I can feel it through my hand. I turn my head and see that her face is pale and laced with shock. I draw her back away and out of the view of the river. She stares up at me, her glassy eyes hold such fear.

"This is a bad idea," I say, tugging on her arm. "We should go back to the house."

Hildy stands her ground. "No," she says, shaking her head. She steps around me and moves back to the top of the rise and stares down at the water. "I ... I need to stay. I promised myself I will never let him win. He will never control anything I do." Her breath comes out hard and fast. The pain is evident in her eyes.

I stand there watching her fight the demon within, knowing from experience that it won't be as easy as she thinks. I know the visions of that day will crush her mind. They will weaken her until she is defeated entirely once again. I cannot do this. I cannot go back down that path.

As I look down at my feet, soft raindrops begin to fall.

"Toby." She turns her face towards me.

I meet her eyes.

"Do you ever think we will be the same? I'd like to think one day it will be possible." Tears roll down over her cheeks.

"Hey, come here." I step in close and stretch my protective arms around her. She offers no resistance as she falls against me. Her head rests against my chest as she breaks down and sobs.

The rain comes in gentle waves as we stand there clinging to each other. All the shame and the guilt I've carried with me for all these years finally releases. My salty tears mingle with the rain. And, as if somehow echoing our pain, the clouds above burst, and a steady drizzle blurs the scene.

For the longest time, we stand there holding each other.

"I'm so sorry, Hildy." I break into the silence. "I'm sorry I couldn't stop him."

She leans back and looks up at me through wet lashes. "It's not your fault what happened to me, Toby. We were only kids."

I turn my head away and look towards the river even though it's no longer visible through the rain.

"Look at me, Toby." Hildy cups her hands on the sides of my face. "Never think that. I saw your battered face, your beaten body that day. You did everything you could to stop him. I recognise that, and you need to understand that too." She blinks away the rivers of rain rolling down over her face. "We did nothing wrong."

Standing there, looking at her, I listen to my breath flow in and out of my lungs. Her words, after all these years, prompt me to look at the situation from a different angle. I was a skinny, awkward, seventeen-year-old boy. What did I expect that boy to have done differently? There was nothing else he could have done. That boy was at an unfair disadvantage from the start against a grown sturdy man. Then, after all the years of beating myself up over the attack, I finally release and let go of everything by forgiving myself.

23

We set out for the river. With every step, the wet sand clings to the sides of our shoes. And just like that, there's a sense of attachment that settles around me. The current carries the essence of my childhood—learning to swim and fish with my father. Catching tadpoles. Making mud pies with Bill. That first day here with Hildy.

I turn my head. Hildy's eyes meet mine.

"After all these years," she says. "I've forgotten what it's like to be out in the rain." She drops her head back, closes her eyes, and lets the droplets splash over her face.

My eyes follow the movement of the water trickling down over her neck, down over the waterlogged dress that clings tightly to her body, exposing the curves of her round, shapely breasts. My breath catches in my throat as I begin to wonder what it would feel like to touch her in ways I've never ventured to before—to caress her bare skin, to engulf my senses with the warmth of her body fitting perfectly against mine. Just thinking about it makes the excitement surge, and I have to look away. Closing my eyes, I allow the rain to wash away my unrealistic thoughts.

Thicker drops now.

The simple touch of her hand makes my insides jump as I'm drawn back into the moment. I turn my head, our eyes lock.

"There are so many things I wish I still had in my life, Toby."

On impulse, the words spray out of my mouth. "Stay. Please don't go tomorrow."

"I can't." She blinks the water away from her eyes. "We both know that I have to go back."

"No, you don't. You can stay here with me."

She lowers her head. "I can't, Toby."

I turn into her. Guiding my hand in under her chin, I lift her face. For a long moment, we just stare at one another. I reach up and tuck her wet hair behind her ear, allowing my fingertips to reacquaint themselves with the side of her face. One touch and the intoxication begins. To be able to make contact with her like this feels as if I've finally exhaled after holding my breath for all these years. I move in closer, feeling the warmth of her body through her wet clothes, which are like a second skin. With that, her breathing becomes harder. Her eyes now carry the same desire as my own.

The downpour is steady now as I trace my fingers down over her neck. She closes her eyes and drops her head back a fraction. "I've wanted to touch you from the moment I saw you," I whisper. "I have loved you every minute of every day. You are the love of my life."

She looks back at me. Her breath comes out in hard visible puffs as tiny water droplets ride through the air. Leaning in, I taste her wet lips, softly and slowly at first, absorbing all their flavour. Then, all at once, her shoulders slump and her body falls into mine as if she's melting from the inside out. My senses tune into every detail—the smell of the storm moving around us, the sweet floral scent of her rain-soaked hair, the electricity playing over our skin.

Suddenly, overhead, lightning cuts through the sky. It's followed by a rolling clap of thunder that's so powerful the earth vibrates under our feet. The wind rushes in and howls, sending the rain pelting down at odd angles.

She pulls back. "I think we need to go."

"Yes, I think so." I slip my hand into hers, pulling her along through the sheeting rain.

As we run through the valley of flowers, the thick mass of rain obscures our view. Within seconds, another rolling boom of thunder reverberates overhead. Hildy lets out a squeal.

"Are you okay?" I yell through the pouring rain.

"Yes! It just scared me."

By the time we make it up to the front porch, an additional bolt of lightning cracks open the sky. Rain hammers down like bullets to the ground. The rolling thunder prompts all the windows in the house to shake. We stand there for the moment, catching our breaths.

"I'm sorry we got caught out in the rain," I say, running my hands back through my hair, feeling the wetness. I glance over to Hildy only to find her eyes are already fixed on me. There's something about the way she's looking at me that causes my heart to pound in my chest. I swallow nervously.

"No need to be sorry. I don't think I have ever felt as alive as I do at this moment." Her gaze slips down to my transparent shirt.

Time seems to slow as I stand there watching the water droplets cling to the end of her lashes before gravity quickly snatches them away. I love you, I tell her silently. I can't let go of you now.

Lightning splits the sky again.

"Here, let me get something to dry off with." I move quickly across the front porch and make my way inside.

From outside, Hildy yells out something, but in all the storm's fury, I don't quite hear what she says. After grabbing the quilt from the back of the lounge, I turn back and notice Hildy is now standing inside the door.

I move swiftly and wrap the quilt around her shoulders. She tilts her head back and stares straight into my eyes. I stop breathing, my pulse pounds.

She lifts her hand and presses her trembling finger to my lips. "Touch me, Toby," she whispers, leaning in to meet my lips.

All previous thoughts evaporate. Now there is only desire. Wrapping my arm around her, I pull her in and taste her mouth. To touch her again is a memory overlapping real time. My lips start the lazy journey down over her neck. "Let me know when you want me to stop," I whisper in between breaths.

"I don't."

I pull back, assuming I have crossed some line. "I'm sorry."

"No. I mean I don't want you to stop."

I swallow and shift from foot to foot. "Are you sure? You don't have to do this you know." My voice breaks a little.

"I know. But I want to. We don't have tomorrow, Toby, so, yes. Yes, I'm sure." She lifts the quilt from her shoulders. It puddles on the floor around her feet.

Each hair on my body stands on end the minute she starts unbuttoning her dress. Every open gap teases. I drink in the sight of her small, firm breasts, her hourglass waist. As the last button opens, my heartrate increases. She stands before me. I lower my glance and take my first glimpse of her naked body, knowing that I will never be the same.

She steps in close to me. My hand automatically drifts down onto her hip, pulling her in. I prop my head against her forehead, closing my eyes. I want to remember this moment, the anticipation of what's about to come. Just to have her near and naked makes it harder for me to breathe.

She reaches out and starts undressing me, beginning first with my shirt. The sensation of her fingers brushing against my skin is imprinted into my mind, my heart. It brings to the surface a desire of need, a passion of want. I battle for control, knowing that I must be gentle with her. I cannot provoke any memory from the past.

Goosebumps form as she slides her hand over my warm, bare skin, touching, discovering, tracing her fingers across the ridges and muscles in my chest. Opening my eyes, I give her a deep, drugging kiss. My hands venture their way around her body, exploring. I want to hold her tight and never let go. My hand steers behind her back as I scoop her up off her feet and walk into the middle of the room, lowering her gently down on the rug. She stares up at me as I trace my fingers over her face. She is a gift. A gift I will always cherish for the rest of my life. Tomorrow, and every day after that, this will be the one memory that gets me through the experience of losing her again.

"You are so beautiful," I whisper. "I will never stop loving you." My lips explore her, starting with her face and moving to her neck. As my mouth approaches the peak of her breast, I hear her inhale. I am not nervous, and neither is she. I know precisely where to touch her.

Her hips arch as my hands wander up over her body. She pulls me in tight, closing her mouth over mine, enticing me. Breathing hard, she guides me into her. The sensation ...

the wonder ... I lose myself. We move slowly together as one. The thrill of flesh on flesh makes our bodies drip with desire. She holds me tighter. I kiss her more deeply as I move against her, stronger, harder. Her nails dig deep into my back until the end comes with a shuddering explosion that I never knew could possibly exist.

Breathless, I collapse down on top of her, burying my face in her long, damp hair. Her heart pounds hard against my chest as a mixture of peace and love descends over me. I brush my lips lightly against the side of her neck. "I didn't hurt you, did I?" I move my exhausted body next to her, draping my arm around her waist.

She turns her head. "No, you didn't hurt me," she whispers, pushing my hair back away from my face. She leans in and kisses me.

Drowsy and spent, we lie there, catching our breath as the faded world slowly returns with the tapping sound of heavy rain on the old tin roof.

24

Tangled between two quilts, Hildy sleeps soundly in the comfort of my arms. I, however, cannot relax knowing that, in a few short hours, she will exist only as a vision in my mind. So, I lie there, letting every little detail of her sear itself into my mind, a keepsake to give me strength in those tough times ahead. Hildy makes a noise in her sleep, wriggling in closer to me. As I watch her, I know she is my impossible dream. Her way of life and the world to which she belongs is so different to mine. In an ideal world, our two lives would never have interacted. Our diverging paths and futures were already planned; we just happened to meet at the crossroads of our journeys.

As the morning light illuminates the room, Hildy's eyes flutter open.

"Hey, you." She smiles, drapes her arm around my chest, and slides her feet between my ankles. "How long have you been awake?"

I lean forward and kiss the top of her head. "Not long. Just a little while."

We both remain silent for a while, each absorbed in our own private thoughts. I know without a doubt she holds my happiness, and knowing this makes me tighten my arms protectively around her.

"Hildy, is it wrong that I want you to stay?"

She sits up suddenly and wraps her arms around her legs.

I shift up onto my elbow. "I know how the world works, and I realise I can't give you the life you're used to, but you already know that. I will love you until I can no longer breathe air into my lungs. I want a life with you, the one we spoke about all those years ago."

"I can't do that, Toby."

"Yes, you can." I sit up.

"No, I can't." She frowns slightly as she swings her face away from me.

I hesitate as I try to hold back the feeling of rejection. Hearing it from her feels as if someone has a hold of my heart and is squeezing the life out of it. Stripped bare and turned inside out, I sit there.

When Hildy eventually speaks, there's a different pitch to her voice. "I'm sorry, but I can't do that."

"If it's because of your parents, you need not worry. I'm not a kid anymore. I can handle myself."

"No ... it's ... You don't understand. I ..." She pauses as she looks back at me. Her face is pale. Small tears cling to her lashes.

I lay my hand on her shoulder. "It's all right. I am sorry. I shouldn't have pushed."

"Please don't hate me for going back." She pauses and searches my gaze with a desperate look before binding her arms around me. Her hold is so tight there is literally no space left between us. "I have to go. You don't understand."

"Hey," I whisper, pulling back.

Her arms drop away from me.

I slide my fingers in under her chin, lifting her face, mopping the tears from her cheeks. "That's not possible, Hildy. I could never hate you. Do you remember that first day we met in the street?"

She nods.

"You could have stormed off with the others and never given me a second thought, but you didn't. You gave me a chance, Hildy. And I am grateful for that. You've changed me in ways I never thought possible. And because of you I know what it's like to love another with all my heart and soul. You did that. You let me love you." Tears form in my eyes, and I immediately blink them away. "I'm not gonna lie. The notion of losing you again, well ... it's gonna kill me, but if that's what you want, then I'll just have to accept that." I twist up the edges of my mouth in a bit of a smile. Her sad gaze holds mine. "At least this time we get to say goodbye." I touch the side of her face. "We didn't get that opportunity last time."

She leans up to meet my lips. "Love me one more time, Toby," she whispers.

I kiss her then, softly at first, and then the taste of passion fuels our bodies. The urgency, the tangled hands, the kisses, the essential embraces, knowing this is the very last time that either one of us will be able to touch the other.

Later that morning, as Hildy showers, I sit and wait for her in the kitchen. Through the open window, I take in the vibrant day outside, the cloudless sky, the sun dusting its warm rays over the earth, the birds chanting with such delight for the glorious day ahead. As I glance back down at the table in front of me, I can't help but smirk at the irony, considering all the misery and sadness I feel inside.

The moment I hear footsteps coming down the hall, I hoist my head up. A second later, Hildy shows up in the doorway. She's dressed again in her yellow frock. Her hair is pinned up underneath her hat. As she pulls on her long white gloves, I notice that the carefree girl with the wild, untamed hair, who was here only minutes ago, has now transformed into a lady of society. When she looks up, she uses her hand to smooth the invisible creases over the front of her dress.

"Okay. I think I'm ready to go now."

My world spins in circles as I get up from the chair. I take her hand in mine and move through the house.

As I close the front door behind me, Hildy waits over near the steps. Her eyes scan the scenery.

As soon as I join her, she whips her head around. "Toby, tell me something I can hold onto."

I draw in a deep breath and take her hand, turning it this way than that. "Whenever you wish to be back here, just look to the moon and know that I am there with you, watching it too."

She smiles and takes in a ragged breath as the tears form in her eyes. She studies my face.

"Why are you looking at me like that?"

"I will always look at you like this."

A tear slides down over her cheek, and I catch it by swiping my fingers lightly over her face. I wrap my arms around her. Every ounce of me never wants to let go.

She pushes away from me.

My hands fall to my sides.

"I wish things were different, Toby, but they aren't. We have to go."

I take her hand. My legs are weak as we move down the steps.

Immersed in the light of the mid-morning sun, the town finally comes into view. In the otherwise empty street, the only sound resonating is the final hymn of the Sunday service. As we proceed down the road, we both remain silent, inspecting every shopfront window we pass. It is then, and twenty yards shy of where we stand, that the church doors burst open. Men, women, and children pile out onto the street. Hildy snatches her hand from mine and retreats a few steps.

"I'm sorry, but if anyone sees me here, especially Mrs. Jessop, my parents will find out, and you know what will take place if they discover where I've been."

When I hear voices from across the street, I shoot my head around and spot Father McGuire standing on the top step. He's smiling, shaking hands, wishing his fellow worshippers a good day as they exit the church.

I quickly turn back to her. "Hey, it's gonna be okay. I'll make sure they don't see you."

"You can't promise that, Toby. Oh, I never should have come back. What was I thinking?" She looks up, and I see the anguish on her face.

"Ah, yes I can. Bill told me years ago to give something a try. So, I'm gonna try it."

"What did he tell you?" Her brows furrow.

"Don't worry. Give me a minute or two before you move down to the train station, and I'll meet you there." I turn my back on her and make my way inconspicuously across the road.

Proper etiquette standards are expected, even from my class of people. And what I am about to do will undoubtedly be the talk of the town for weeks—months even—but I have to do it. I have to get her to the train station unseen.

When I make it over to the other side of the road and reach the footpath, I sprint to the church, waving my hand above my head. "Father McGuire! Father McGuire!" I yell loud enough to make a scene. "Wait, Father McGuire!"

Every face in the crowd shifts towards me. As I move, I look at their faces, the tightness of their features. Some are old family friends. Some are people I went to school with. Every single one of them turned on us years ago, slandering us so we were permanently banished.

"Oh, don't tell me I missed it!" I sing out. "I knew I should have gotten up earlier." People watch me as I move up the steps, their faces stunned. "I couldn't remember if it was nine or ten, but at least I now know for next week." Stopping on the stoop beside Father McGuire, I stare out over the sea of horrified faces. "I was hoping we could have a chat. Lately, I've heard strange voices in my head, and I want to know if there is any way of getting rid of them."

All around me, I hear the whispers. I scratch my head, allowing my eyes to drift back across the street. Hildy's still striding towards the station.

"Toby, I didn't realise you were back." He links his fingers, then rests his hands down on his large belly as he flashes a look out over the crowd. "May I ask what you're doing here?"

I open my mouth to answer, but before I can get a single word, out a voice comes from behind. "It is fine, Father. I can handle it."

Closing my eyes, I stay planted on the spot. I didn't even give Picker a thought when I concocted this idea in my head. Next, I feel his hand pulling me off to one side.

"What are you doing, mate?"

"It's all right," I whisper in close to him. "I'm not going crazy. It's just a decoy so Hildy can get to the station unseen."

"She's back? After all these years?"

"Yeah, and she's worried that someone will see her and report back to her parents. So I'm causing a distraction."

"Well, you'd better sell it, mate."

"That's what I'm trying to do, but you're stopping me."

"Oh, sorry about that." He lets go of my arm. Twisting around, he holds his hands up, surrendering. "Yeah, sorry, Father, but he won't listen to me. From my understanding, Toby was hoping to be included once again in the parish. Is that right Toby?" He shoots a look back over at me, gives a wink, then retreats back down the steps and weaves his way through the crowd.

Dry-mouthed, I slip my hands into my pockets and peer out at all the disgusted faces. "Yeah, that's right. I am coming back to attend mass every Sunday like I did with my mother when I was little."

"I don't think that would be such a good idea, Toby."

"And why not?"

Looking a little uncomfortable, Father McGuire shifts on his feet. "There is a reason that your family hasn't been a part of this congregation, and I think you know what that is."

"And, do you honestly think you can stop me from turning up next week?"

"You seem to forget that I can have you removed from my church." His voice rises to an uncomfortable pitch. A blue vein bulges in his forehead. "You hear me!" He pauses and straightens his shoulders to regain his composure.

I cast my eyes over the street. Hildy is gone. "Yeah, I hear ya. But ..." I move down the stairs. The sizeable crowd parts, creating a narrow path for me to walk along. "You won't be able to stop Bill, though. You know how stubborn he is. If he wants to come back, he'll come back. He's already told me he wants to talk about the voices in his head." I pause for effect and turn to face Father McGuire. "It's like that time when you didn't want anyone to know you gave my mother confessional. I clearly remember you saying that you, too, heard the voices in your head."

Every face turns to Father McGuire.

"So maybe Bill and I will be okay because it hasn't affected you yet."

Father McGuire lifts his hands and addresses the rowdy crowd. "He's lying, everyone! He's lying!"

"Oh, well ... if you don't believe me, I suggest you ask Bill next week when he's here. He'll tell you the truth." I walk unnoticed through the confused crowd as every shocked glance homes in on Father McGuire where he stands at the top of the steps. Some faces have turned white. Some people hold their hands up over their gaping mouths in disbelief. I knew it was a sin to lie, but after the way he treated my mother, I didn't care.

"It's all a lie I tell you!" Father McGuire's voice sounds from behind. "It's a lie."

As soon as I leave the crowd behind, I lift my head to the heavens. "You were right! It is fun. I only wish you were here to enjoy it."

By the time I arrive at the end of the street, the train has pulled into the station and is coming to a shuddering halt. Grey steam spews out of the stacks. Carriage doors open, and passengers by the dozens, pile out. Some carry suitcases while others hold small children. I scan the platform for Hildy, but with all the travellers it's impossible to spot her yellow dress. I cross over to the left, climb up onto the bench seat, and squint out over all the moving heads. There, at the end of the platform, I find her standing alone.

Despite the anguish of letting her go, I charge my way through the crowd. Along the way, I wonder how I will do this. How can I say goodbye to a person who will forever be a part of me?"

When I approach, she lifts her head. Her eyes are glassy. Her face is mangled with such sorrow. My first inclination is to wrap my arms around her, but the minute I step forward, she presses her palm against my chest, stopping me.

"Don't." She glances about. "Someone might see us."

I lower my hands down to my sides and peer back over my shoulder.

The platform is alive with activity. Suitcases are being stacked onto the train. Children are chasing each other, darting in and around loved ones as they whisper their goodbyes.

When the whistle sounds signalling the five-minute departure warning, I whip my head around. Hildy blinks, but her tears escape and slide down over her cheeks. She doesn't bother to wipe them away. I watch her fight, knowing she isn't as robust as she pretends to be. She shakes her head, looks at the train and then down at the ground—anywhere else except in my direction.

"Hildy, I wish you didn't have to—"

"I'm sorry, Toby." She interrupts, stepping forward. "But I have to ..." She chokes herself off and lifts her head, avoiding making eye contact with me. Another flood of tears spill. This time she uses the fingers of her gloves to swipe them away.

"I'm so glad you came back." As I speak, my throat feels as if it's closing. "Hildy, I want you to know that—"

She brushes past me and makes her way to the train.

"Hildy," I add, turning quickly.

She pauses but keeps her back to me.

"I'm always here if you change your mind."

She rushes along the platform, and I wonder if she knows how hard it is for me to let her go.

A few seconds later, she climbs her way up onto the train. Taking a deep breath, I keep my eyes focused on her, just in case she turns around. She doesn't. Instead, she disappears into the belly of the train. I'm dizzy now.

Into the silence, the conductor yells out. "All aboard! The train is about to leave!" The whistle blows once again.

Turning my head, I notice the crowd has thinned on the platform. I fall into a trance-like state as the reality of her leaving sets in.

Grey smoke belches out into the air as the train jerks forward. Then, slowly, it moves. I peer into every passing window, yearning for one last peek of Hildy, but it's difficult to locate her with all the people hanging out through open windows as they wave goodbye to their loved ones left at the station. Another carriage passes, and then another. My chest rises and falls with uneven breaths, and as the train pulls away from the station, I break down as she takes my heart with her.

Unmoving, unblinking, I watch through blurred eyes as the train liquefies into the land. I stay a long time, even after the thumping and rattling sounds dissipate into the distance. I stand there in the silence, in all the doom.

Time passes; I am not sure how much. But when I eventually turn, I am the only soul standing at the station. I start the journey home, but it's going to take me a while because my body and mind are working against each other.

25

It's been three months since I said goodbye to Hildy. That day my heart broke into a thousand pieces, but I suppose that's proof I have loved. Even though our time together was limited, she saved my life. I still carry the pain of that day, but it no longer cripples me in the way it once did. I think I've finally accepted that it happened and that cruel, horrible, unforgiving actions sometimes fall into our lives and shape us into the people we become. But, I survived it, and I am stronger for it. I returned to the river that afternoon after Hildy left, and I've been coming back every afternoon ever since. That sense of belonging is stronger now than it ever was. I think all those wonderful memories that were created here have overshadowed that awful day. Somehow, just being here with the smell of eucalyptus in the air, the sounds of the river, and the sand shifting under my feet, I feel as if all those people I love are still here with me.

As the daylight dwindles into dusk, the air becomes thick with white cockatoos flying overhead. I lift my face and allow my eyes to follow them as they cruise downstream. Across the river, outstretched tree branches sway to the rhythm of the breeze. I kneel down and pluck a thin black pebble out of the sand. Five skips, and then it dives down into the murky water. Wiping my damp fingers down the side of my pants, I give one last look at the river before I make my way home.

When I step into the valley of wildflowers, I stop and slide my hands into my pockets. Taking a deep breath, I stand completely still. There she is again, in the fading light walking through the wildflowers, so beautiful the way her hair hangs down over her shoulders. She's so lifelike that I have to tell myself to breathe. But don't blink, for if I do, I may lose this wonderful hallucination of Hildy. She looks up, shields her eyes from the sun, and smiles. As usual, she walks towards me. I expect any minute now she will dissolve into thin air as she has done so many times before. The image of her lasts a little longer this time. She moves right up in front of me. I want to reach out and touch her. She blinks.

The tears flood my eyes when I comprehend she's not a hallucination. Oh my god! She's real! My arms coil around her.

"I thought I'd find you here." She pulls back and looks up at me.

"What are you doing here?" My eyes roam over her face. I can't stop smiling.

"I just had to come after I read my engagement notice in the paper this morning." She is quiet for a moment, and I watch her inhale. "I told my parents no, but they won't listen. They still insist I marry him."

"So do they know you're here?"

"No, and I don't care." She smiles. "Oh, Toby, I realise now how stupid I've been. In all the years of worrying that you would get into trouble, I forgot how to live. It's so silly of me to think they would have you arrested. They would never want society to find out what happened to me." She retreats a few steps and straightens her shoulders. "There are so many things I've wanted to say to you over the years, but I've never dared to have the courage to say any of it." As our eyes linger, she reaches up and touches her fingers to her flushed cheeks. "Oh, will you look at me? I'm already blushing just thinking about it." She licks her lips and gives a nervous smile. "The last time I said this, it didn't go too well. Anyway, what I'm trying to say is … Oh, why is this so hard?"

"It's okay, Hildy, you don't have to say it."

"Yes! Yes, I do. Now please don't interrupt me until I'm finished. Otherwise, I will never get it out."

"Okay," I say, pursing my lips together.

"Well …" She looks down. "After I went back there, I knew I didn't want that life anymore. Instead, I want the same as you. I want the life we spoke about." She lifts her head. "This place, here with you, feels more like home than any other place I have ever lived. I'm so sick of sleepwalking through my life."

At that precise second, a flock of birds spook and take flight. Hildy pauses, lifts her head, and looks at them for a minute. As soon as she loses sight of them in the dimming sky, she swings her eyes back, and I notice her hands trembling. "Now, where was I? Oh, that's right. When I saw my name printed in black and white next to a complete stranger's name, it finally jolted me into taking control of my life before it's too late. I know what I want."

As she speaks, I feel the wind on my face. I brush my sweaty palms against the sides of my pants.

"I've always known what I want. I was just too scared of the consequences if I went after it. But no more. I choose you, Toby." She moves in close and takes my hand. "I love you." She speaks from the heart. "I've always loved you. It's you who makes me happy. You are the only reason I'm still breathing. I cannot live another day without you." She looks down at our joined hands. "I'm sorry I couldn't say it—"

My heart swells hearing those words. I cut her off by kissing her—a slow, deep kiss as if, somehow, I'm trying to mend the time that's already been lost between us. I settle my hands down on her waist. "I love you too," I whisper.

"I know you do. I always have." She heaves a big sigh. "Gosh, I can't believe I finally said it ..." She trails off. "Now, shall we go home? It's getting late."

"Wait," I say. Hildy stares at me as I kneel down and pluck a wildflower from the ground.

She smiles, accepts the flower, and threads her arm through mine. Together, we walk home in the fading light. All the years of waiting for her, all the struggles that led to this moment have all been worth it. I now want for nothing. Everything I could ever want or need is right here at my side.

26

Light explodes into the room. The machines beep loudly.

"Wake up, Mr. Mitchell. Wake up. It's time."

With great effort, I blink as I try to remember where I am. When my mind catches up, I get up from the lounge that has been my bed for the past nine days. I shuffle forward, saying my silent prayer, asking the Lord to take my soul and leave hers alone.

I lift my head and immediately stop as I take sight of the tubes weaving in and out her body. No matter how many times I've seen them, it still haunts me. My only hope is that my mind is strong enough to dissolve these final images of her.

The day the doctor told us the cancer had come back, we never spoke about what would happen the day death would arrive to collect her. Instead, we wanted to bask in the memory of our youth, to look back by retelling our stories and remembering all those who have passed before us. She did most of the talking, as usual. All I wanted to do was hold her, knowing she would soon leave my side.

Sensing the nurse is watching me, I turn my head and meet her prying eyes. Her face is without its usual smile.

"Are you okay, Mr. Mitchell?" she asks. "Do you need some help?"

"I'm fine," I lie. I know I haven't fooled her, but I nod anyway, glancing back over to Hildy.

When I reach the side of her bed, my chest tightens. It's torture seeing her this way. The process of dying is cruel, but it's one we all must undertake at some point. Our time is limited. No one knows when those final hours will come. But when it does, and you're standing there in front of your maker, it won't matter who you are. It doesn't matter if you had an extravagant house or a tremendous amount of money. No. All you'll be asking is, did I get it right? Did I make the most of my messed-up life? Did I love enough? Was I kind? Did I hold onto what really matters?

Placing my hand down on top of hers, I feel the coldness in her fingers. This is it. This is actually happening. I do nothing but stare at her beautiful face, noting how the years have changed her. Every line displays a remarkable chapter of our glorious life together. And still, even after all these years, I can catch glimpses of that sixteen-year-old girl who captured my heart. My love for her is and will be everlasting, just as the wedding bands on our fingers. Although they may appear worn and tarnished, our love for each other has never wavered. She is still my perfect dream, my home, the light in all the dark. I know I have been the luckiest man on this earth to have loved her in all her forms. And even though she will no longer be at my side, I will continue to love her in that form as well. Tomorrow, if I do not wake, I will not care, for she is the only reason my heart still beats.

I lift my face and look to the vase of wildflowers Tristan brought in for her this morning. I close my eyes, shutting my eyelids tight. My head pounds. My heart aches. There are still too many things I need to say to her. I open my eyes and lean forward, pressing my lips to the back of her hand, knowing this will be our last touch. She looks so small and frail, half the size of the woman I know. Staring, I reach across and stroke her soft, grey hair, wondering if she even knows I am still here, for I haven't seen those beautiful green eyes for a while now.

Her breath comes in shallowed jagged spurts.

I lift my face to the nurses surrounding the bed. "Is she in pain?"

"No, Mr. Mitchell, she isn't." Whispers one of them. "It will be over soon."

My conflicting emotions keep me silent. My shaky legs are like water underneath me. There's an icy numbness that swirls through my soul, as if a part of me is dying too. There is no way I can stop the tears.

All of a sudden, an unbearably loud, high-pitched noise pierces through the room. The nurses jolt into action. One works quickly to silence the machines while the other steps forward, grabbing Hildy's wrist, to check for a pulse.

None of them say anything right away. As the long seconds tick by, the wait torments every inch of me. I open my mouth to inquire, but the tears come too fast, fleeing my eyelids, separating into every wrinkle. Through blurred vision, I keep focusing on the nurse in front of me, and although I cannot see her face, I pre-empt what she's about to say. No, don't say it. Don't say it. I don't want to hear those words. As I wait, I swallow. My throat feels as if it's about to close.

She lifts her head. "I'm sorry, Mr. Mitchell, but she has passed."

The pain of hearing those words squeezes in on my heart. I hunch over as the air bolts out of my lungs.

"Are you okay, Mr. Mitchell?" The nurses scurry around to my side of the bed. Grabbing me by the arms, they steady me, ease me back over to the lounge.

I sit. I lose all aspect of time, and everything happens in slow motion. I watch numbly as one of the nurses turns and crosses the room. She stops at the bedside table and pulls open the bottom drawer. I wonder if she's packing up Hildy's things. I want to yell out and tell her to stop and bugger off because I am not ready to leave Hildy just yet, but I can't make the words form in my mouth.

The other nurse stoops down into my personal space, blocking my view. Her mouth is moving, but with all the fog in my head, I can't seem to hear what she is saying. I just want her to get out of the way so I can see what the other nurse is doing.

Finally, she clears out of the way and I catch the other nurse walking towards me. "This is for you, Mr. Mitchell," she says, extending her hand.

I stare up at her through misty eyes. Then, ever so slowly, my gaze slides down to the white envelope in her hand. I swallow. It's a little while before I speak. "I don't understand."

"It's from Mrs. Mitchell. She made all of us promise that, on the day of her passing, we would give this to you."

I look up, confused, as if somehow doubting if I heard right. I begin to wonder if I'm making it all up in my head.

A second nurse leans in, shoving her face again into mine. "Do you need a glass of water?"

"No, I don't need any water," I snap, leaning back in the lounge. I take a breath realising my tone may have been a little sharp. "I'm sorry." I give a slight smile and look back at the envelope. "How long has the letter been there?"

"Since the day Mrs. Mitchell was admitted. She said it was imperative that we give it to you, but if it's too hard—"

"No! No," I add too quickly. "It's not too hard. It's just ... Well, I don't think I can read at the moment, with my eyes the way they are. Could you read it to me please?"

For a few seconds, she stares down at the envelope in her hand and breathes deeply. Then, turning it, she pries it open with her fingers. She removes the letter, unfolds it, and in a soft voice, she reads aloud ...

My dearest Toby

Our time together has been the most magical ride I could have wished for. You and I were born into very different worlds and, over the years, many ignorant people have reminded us of that, but what those naïve people didn't seem to understand is that you changed me for the better. That first day, when you dared to approach, you opened up a new world I never knew existed. You freed my spirit that day. I've never told you this before, but that day down at the river, you made such an impact on me. I was never the same. You revealed there was more to life than wealth and greed.

Over the years, I know you often wondered if I ever regretted giving up my old life. The answer is no—never! Why would I choose a life in which I just existed? You have given me the most marvellous, spectacular gift any one individual can give another. So, thank you for our glorious, remarkable life. I've told you often that love did not exist in my family. I didn't know what love was until the moment you walked into my life. It was you who taught me. And because of that, I now know what it feels like to have a person love me entirely for who I am, and how it is to love another with all my heart and soul. I now know that the concept of losing a love is much like death itself. And that is the reason I had to pen this letter to you.

Some people wander through their lives in a daze, never experiencing a fraction of the love we shared. No amount of money could ever produce the beautiful life we made together. And, if I had the chance to do it all again, I would choose you in a heartbeat.

Together, we have endured our darkest hours, always at the hands of others, but the one thing I want you to know is that you are the person who mended my soul. You were and still are the most significant gift I could ever want. I have never loved another person the way I still love you.

We have been ripped apart so many times, and every time we have found our way back to each other. And in my heart, I know this is another one of those times. So until then—until we see our way back—I want you to do something for me. I want you to pick the wildflowers, dance in the rain, and watch every sunset, for I will be there with all the loved ones who have passed before me. Promise me, Toby. Promise me you will live your remaining days here on this earth with love, happiness, and joy, knowing when it is time to meet your maker, you gave it all with no regrets.

You are my best friend, my one and only love.
Forever yours,
Hildy

When she finishes with the letter, she looks up. Oddly, her eyes are filled with tears. "Mrs. Mitchell truly loved you, didn't she?" Her voice changes.

"That she did, and I love her too."

She pauses to wipe her tears. A moment later, she holds the letter out in front.

As I take it, a lump appears in the back of my throat as I catch sight of the familiar, curvy scroll. I look up at her. "Thank you for reading the letter." I get up from the lounge and shuffle my way back across the room. When I reach Hildy's side, I rest my hands down on the bed and stare at her beautiful face. For the longest time, I think about her letter. I think about that first day when I plucked up the courage to approach her. I think about all the kisses and the embraces we have shared over the years that built a lifetime of happiness, a life of wonder. I think about how our beautiful life seemed to pass like a shadow. I lean forward. There's such sadness in my heart. "As usual, you are right, my dear. We will see each other again. We always do. So, until then, I promise to pick the wildflowers, to dance in the rain. And know that I will be waiting there every day to say hello." I touch her ageless lips against my own, knowing this is the very last time. The mist grows in my eyes. "Thank you for letting me love you. I, too, have had the most incredible ride."

I straighten up my crooked body, and with extreme care, I fold the letter in half, place it back into the envelope, and safely secure it down into my pocket so I can read it over and over again.

The End

Book 2 - Cherish The Wildflowers out 2022

Thank you ♡

Pick The Wildflowers has been a joy to write. To all the readers out there, I don't know how to express my deepest love for you. You take a chance on my books every time I release a new one, which is something I can never show enough gratitude for. So thank you for being the best fans a girl can ask for. You make my job so much fun.

Thank you to my husband Stephen and my two boys, Bailey and Toby. You always believe in me - that is the most significant gift you could ever give me.

Thank you to my mum, Marilyn, who always reads my messy first drafts. Your feedback is always appreciated.

About the Author

Tracy is an Australian Author. She is drawn to writing about characters who feel powerless by those challenging moments that life offers. She likes to mix dark with the light and push her characters through the highs and lows so that the reader feels moved by the story.
Want to keep up to date with any new releases or find out about fun giveaways. Then sign up for Tracy's newsletter or follow her on social media.

http://tracyleethompsonauthor.com/
or
 @tracyleethompsonauthor

Book Club Kit

Questions for Discussion

① The Novel begins with the main character, Toby, thinking back to the first time he saw Hildy. What impact did she have on him?

② How did Bill falling in love with Hildy affect Toby?

③ Who loved Hildy more, Bill or Toby and how was their love different?

④ How did the mother's illness affect the two boys?

⑤ Do you think the social standings still exist today?

⑥ How do you think Hildy's attack impacted Toby?

⑦ Whilst reading this novel, did you think Toby could find someone else and suppress his love for Hildy?

⑧ Did you predict the ending?

⑨ What do you think Hildy's parents will do now?

⑩ Do you think Pick The Wildflowers is the best name for this book? If not, what else could it have been called?

A Conversation with
Tracy Lee Thompson

How did you come up with Pick The Wildflowers?

The first spark of this story came to me in a vivid dream. An elderly man, named Toby Mitchell, was narrating his life. In this dream, I saw visuals in colour and, felt the atmosphere as if I was there.

The next day, I couldn't stop thinking about the dream. I put on hold my current work in progress and began jotting down the things I had seen. Over time, the dream came back, and when it did, it continued on from exactly where it had left off. It was as if someone had pressed the play button to view a movie.

Did you do any research?

Yes, a little. I had to make sure I did this story justice. For my research, I travelled to the Australian War Memorial to investigate the Pacific War. I studied up on the 1930-40's. But the heart of the story is love. The love of a family bond. The love of a person who owns your heart. Toby's story is one of hardship, rejection and regret. We can all relate to those aspects of life. But overall, it is love and the way he looks at life that gets him through those darkest moments. Writing his story made me look at my own life. Now, every day I am grateful for the life I have and the people who share it with me and all those I meet along the way.

Did you have any challenges when writing this story?

Yes. Even though I was keen to put pen to paper and jot down everything I had seen in the dream. I was worried that when I wrote all the devastating moments, I wouldn't be able to capture the gentle side of Toby. That I wouldn't be able to deliver the way he and Bill looked at life. But it was those heart-wrenching moments that were such a challenge for me. During the first draft, I had to walk away as I did nothing but cry. As time went on, I thought it would get easier, but it didn't. Still today, I cannot read this story without tearing up.

Do you plan on writing any more stories about Toby and Hildy?

Yes. I am in the process of writing the next two novels. There is still so much to write about their life together and the external challenges they face along the way.

If you enjoyed *Pick The Wildflowers,* you'll love Tracy Lee Thompson's

Follow The Stars

Set in 1925, the betrayal of her parents shocks seventeen-year-old, Evie Brown. Stubborn, quick-tempered Evie must now face the frightful reality of her new life as she adjusts to the harsh demands of a wealthy, aristocratic family, the McCormicks. They are now her greatest enemy, especially the eldest son, Vincent.

As Evie suffers at the hands of Vincent's cruel ways, Flynn McCormick, (the second-born son - who in his parent's eyes will never be as good as Vincent) tries to protect her.

Despite Evie's reservations, she lowers her guard and accepts Flynn's help. By doing so, Evie's love for Flynn unravels. Not only has she fallen in love with the enemy, but Flynn has also set off a dream that she can follow the stars. But the simple fact of who she is and where she comes from still haunts her. People like her never get a chance to dream.

AVAILABLE IN EBOOK AND PAPERBACK NOW

Turn the page for
a sneak peek from

Follow The Stars

1925

Chapter One

Evie

I am awoken by the chill of the frosty morning. Once again, the harsh night has sucked all the warmth right out of the house. I know I have to get up and tend to the fire, but the thought of the frigid air closing its icy claws around me makes me stay in my bed a little longer. I draw in a long slow breath, pull the covers under my chin and sleepily gaze around the room.

Darkness still whispers in all of the corners. Patches of ice lay frozen to the windows. Through the opaque window, the outside world slowly materialises. Angry, bloated clouds hang low in the sky. It's already a month into spring. When will winter's frosty bite ever end?

As I lay there, my mind conjures up another fairy-tale I can relay to my little brother, Leo, who has just turned six. He adores my stories, unlike my little sister, Maggie, who is now eight. I'm pretty sure she doesn't like my stories because they scare her. Every morning while I prepare breakfast, Leo sits at the table and listens. Over the years, my mother has told me that my horrid stories, as well as my temper, will get me into trouble.

I know it's my responsibility to look after Leo and Maggie, not because my mother told me to, but because I am the eldest. Ever since they were born, I have loved them with all my heart. Over the years, I've often wondered if I need Maggie and Leo more than they actually need me.

When I can't stand the cold any longer, I toss back the blanket and jump out of bed. Every hair on my body stands on end as the goosebumps surge across my skin. I quickly dress and then race barefoot across the chilly floorboards out towards the kitchen.

As soon as I burst through the open doorway, my mother is bent over at the fireplace, jabbing the iron poker into the coals. With a quick turn of her head, she acknowledges my arrival.

"Well, don't just stand there gawking. Get some twigs."

Immediately, I race to the basket of wood near the side door. Seconds later, I am standing next to my mother with an armful of twigs. While I wait patiently for more instructions, I watch the thin wisps of smoke lift and curl as the tiny flames strain to stay alight.

"Righto," my mother says, stepping back. "Throw them in now."

Within seconds, the new flames dance and pulsate to life. Twigs crackle and pop as ample heat gushes out. I hold my palms up towards the flames to welcome the warmth.

"So, did you wash your hair like I asked?" I can't help but notice there's an edge to my mother's voice.

"Yes, I did," I reply, unconsciously running my fingers through my long brown hair. I wonder why she's been so adamant about me washing my hair. She has never insisted on it before. I always keep it clean.

I turn my head to see her studying me. I recognise the look. It's the look I've been getting for the past three days. Under her intense stare, I pull my cardigan a little tighter in around my middle. Something is up. For the past week, she's been distant. She's been so short with me. I do not know what I've done. No matter how hard I try to please her, she always gets that look on her face. That sharp tone in her voice. Without saying another word, she turns and leaves the room.

I think about the past few days, wondering why my mother is so cross with me. Did I not do enough chores around the house? No, that can't be it because I've done everything that I usually do. A thought pops into my head. It's the ribbons. That's what it has to be. That's when everything changed. I should never have mentioned anything about wanting a pair of red ribbons for my seventeenth birthday. I lean forward, grab a block of wood from out of the basket, and shove it into the fire. When Mother returns, I will let her know that it's okay that I didn't get anything on my birthday. I know money is scarce and that we've none to spare. Surely that will get things back to the way they were.

The old floorboards creak behind me. I keep my eyes focused on the fire in front because I know exactly who it is. It's my little brother, Leo. Every morning, for the past two months, Leo's been trying to scare me. Most mornings, I let him think he's the nimble panther who is light on his feet, which, of course, he isn't, but still, I pretend to be surprised by his sudden appearance.

Another sound from the floorboards lets me know he's close. Out of the corner of my eye, I watch him. He stands still for the moment, as if contemplating his next move, then shifts forward. When he's about to reach out and touch me, I spin around in a sneak attack.

Leo screams and laughs out loud. "You scared me, Evie."

Laughing, I scoop him up off the floor. "I know. I saw you jump."

He puts his arms around my neck and hugs me tight. "Do you have a story to tell me today?"

"Of course, I do."

Leo wrestles free from my arms. The second his feet hit the floor, he races over to sit in a chair at the table.

From off the top shelf, I grab a pot to prepare the porridge. "Okay, are you ready, Leo?" I look back over my shoulder to see him nod. "Once in a land that lay far across the shining seas, there lived a prince, but he did not know he was a prince."

"Why didn't he know?"

"Because they took him from the King's castle when he was only a tiny baby," I emphasise each word to make it sound more exciting. "The King's men search all the lands, even the dark forest for years, but he was never found."

"Who took him?"

When I look back at Leo, my younger sister, Maggie, is standing by the doorway, rubbing her sleepy eyes.

"It's cold," she complains. "Didn't anyone get up to put wood on the fire?"

"Shhh!" Leo spits in Maggie's direction. "Evie is telling me a story."

"Oh, be quiet, Leo. Why can't you just shut up for once?" Maggie strides across to the table. "You know I don't like Evie's stories."

"Well, I do, so be quiet."

"No, you be quiet and stop wearing my favourite socks."

"I didn't wear your socks."

"Yes, you did. I saw that you had them on yesterday."

"I showed you those socks, and they weren't yours."

"That's enough, you two," I say, stirring the porridge. "Leo, we'll finish the story after breakfast."

"No, Evie. I want to hear it now."

"After breakfast, I promise."

Leo looks to Maggie, who sits in the chair opposite him at the table. "You always ruin everything."

I don't even realise my mother is back in the room until I hear her barking orders. "Maggie, get your elbows off the table. Leo, sit up straight. You two stop the bickering. Evie, where's your hairbrush?"

I look back over at my mother. She's holding a small carpetbag in her hands.

"Your hairbrush Evie. Quick I don't have all day."

Distracted by the bag in her hands, it takes me a few seconds to answer. "Ahhh... It's on the windowsill. Why do you need –" But before I can attempt to finish the sentence, my mother turns away and moves down the hall.

I turn back to stir the porridge. What's with the bag? Why does she need my hairbrush? Then it clicks. My cheeks flush. There is a flutter of panic in my stomach as I drop the spoon onto the counter and go in search of her.

My heart thumps at an alarming rate when I discover she's in my bedroom. I have so many questions, yet I can't find my tongue to ask any of them. I glance over to the windowsill. The brush is gone. Anxiety tingles through my chest as I wait for my mother to tell me what is going on.

I watch her move about the room. She grabs my nightgown from off the bed and stuffs it into the bag.

"What are you doing?" I ask shakily. "Why are you putting all my things in there?" I follow her around the room as she continues to stuff more of my belongings into the bag. My skin prickles. I'm frantic to know what the hell is going on. Fists clenched, I scream at her. "Tell me why you've got my stuff!"

My harsh tone stops her in her tracks. She turns and glares at me. "How many times have I told you about that temper?"

Wordlessly, she tosses a look around the room, and then as if satisfied everything is packed, she closes the sides of the bag and looks up. "Is that porridge I smell burning?"

I push past her and race back to the kitchen. Hands shaking, I grab the pot off the stove.

The sight of my mother walking back into the kitchen and dropping the bag near the front door triggers panic. I grab two bowls from out of the cupboard and start scooping out the porridge, careful not to scrape any of the burnt bits stuck to the bottom. A surge of tears comes to my eyes, knowing my mother doesn't want me here. I hold steady, trying with all my might to quickly blink them away. Where am I supposed to go?

"Is the porridge ready, Evie?" asks Leo.

I wipe my face and take a steady breath before I turn.

As soon as I reach the table, Leo and Maggie pick up their spoons. The second I put the bowls down in front of them, they start burrowing into their breakfast. As I take a few steps back from the table, my eyes automatically shift to the bag by the front door.

"Can you tell me what is going on?" I ask, peering up at my mother. "Why did you put my stuff in there?" The anxiety tingles in my chest.

Her quiet, harsh stare makes me a little nervy, but I hold firm, keeping my eyes on her. The seconds tick. And still, she does not answer. I bite down on my bottom lip to stop the rising anger from spewing out. All I want to do is scream at her to tell me what the hell is going on.

The short sharp tap on the front door startles me.

"Who's that?" I ask.

"Never you mind. Just be on your best behaviour and control that temper, Evie." She moves quickly across the room. She rests her hand on the doorknob, takes a deep breath, and then pulls the door open.

"Hello, we've been expecting you,' she says in a cheery, upbeat voice.

Standing in the open doorway is a man dressed all in black. He looks a little out of place in his long overcoat, expensive suit and hat. Behind him, there is a shiny black car parked out in the street.

"Please come in," my mother says. She steps off to one side and sweeps her hand before the open room.

The man quickly removes his fedora before stepping in and looking around. I cringe the second his eyes fall on me.

"Is this the girl?" His assessing gaze travels down over my frame. "Is this Evie?"

My skin contracts when he says my name. *Who is this man? And how does he know my name?*

"Yes, that's her," my mother adds, closing the front door.

"Good, Good. Mrs McCormick will be pleased."

Mrs McCormick. Who the hell is Mrs McCormick? I peer across to my mother, who has not moved from the front door. "What is going on?" I tug slightly on the front of my dress.

"You haven't told her?" The stranger turns to gaze at my mother.

"No," I add, my voice rising to an uncomfortable pitch. "She hasn't told me anything. She's only packed up my things." I look at the stranger. "I have no idea who you are or what you're doing here."

At the table, Maggie shoves her bowl forward and gets down from the chair. I turn and watch her leave the room. When I look back, the stranger has already circled the table and is moving towards me. My breath catches in my throat.

"It's okay, Evie," he says. "I'll tell you everything in a minute. First, I need to do a few assessments as per Mrs McCormick's request." He stops in front of me, opens his jacket and reaches inside the breast pocket. He pulls out a thin metal rod.

Unbelievable images enter my mind. My eyes flicker to the rod in his hand. "What are you doing with that?"

"Relax. It will not hurt you," the stranger adds in a soft voice. "On Mrs McCormick's orders, I need to do a thorough inspection before this goes ahead."

"Before what goes ahead?" I snap my head round to stare at my mother. She has her head shunted off to one side. "Why won't you look at me? Just tell me what's going on." I stand there, willing her to answer.

My mother rushes across the room. Her fierce eyes lock onto mine. "You are old enough to leave home. Your father has secured a good job for you. Now do as this man says."

My mouth falls open. I'm not even sure if I've heard right. Totally stunned, I stand there, blinking a few times, trying to clear the fog that's just entered my brain. How long have the two of them planned this? Weeks. Months. Years? I feel sudden lightheadedness and panic as I look at Leo, who still sits at the table, eating his breakfast. How can I ever leave him? How can I ever leave Maggie? The tears swell in my eyes. We're all supposed to grow up together. I bite down on my tongue to stop myself from crying.

"Surely, you must have known you couldn't stay here forever," says my mother.

"I'll eat less. I promise. Please don't make me go," I blurt out. "I promise I'll do more. Please, I beg you." My lip trembles. "Please, Mum. Please, don't make me go."

She studies me for the moment. The time and silence stretch before her face softens. Just when I think she's about to reconsider, she straightens up and marches forward. "Lower your head so the man can check for lice." She turns to the man. "Whenever you're ready."

Her words feel as if they've physically slapped the side of my face. My mind goes into overdrive. Did my mother and father not love me? Was I nothing but a burden to them?

"Lower your head now," my mother demands. "The quicker we get this over with, the better it will be for everyone."

My scalp tingles as I come to realise I've no choice in the matter. This is happening to me whether or not I like it. Shocked, I continue to stare at her through blurred eyes.

"Get your head down now," she demands, yanking my arm to pull me in front of the stranger.

"It's all right, Mrs Brown," the stranger says. "I'm sure Evie can do this herself."

Through misty eyes, I stare up at him.

"Are you ready?"

I nod in a jerky fashion, unable to find any words because I'm horrified it has come down to this. My family, who are supposed to love me, prefer not to have me here anymore.

"Okay, look down, Evie. It won't take long."

I drop my chin down to my chest and stare at the floor. The thin metal rod lifts small sections of my long, thick hair. I press my lips tightly together and stare at the two shiny black shoes moving around me. I think about Maggie and wonder if this too is to be her fate just days after her seventeenth birthday. And Leo. My sweet little brother. My chest tightens as I wonder if in years to come if he will even remember me. The tears swell in my eyes. With a quick swipe of my fingers, I brush them away.

"Well," says the stranger. "Everything seems to be in order."

I lift my head and push my hair back from my face to see the man sliding the metal rod back into his jacket pocket.

"So, you're all good to go then," says my mother.

A wave of anger snakes its way up to the surface. "I can't believe you did this." I spit each word out through gritted teeth. "I thought parents were supposed to love their children. How stupid of me to think that." I turn my madness onto the stranger. "How dare you come here and do that. You're just as bad as her. And you..." My attention snaps back to my mother. "I loved you. I can't understand why you did this. You're callous. Cold-hearted. That's what you are." I glare at her as the tears stream down my face.

"It's not like that, Evie," my mother says.

When she reaches out to touch me, I turn away and push past her. "Don't even bother. Nothing will ever change what you did." I walk over to Leo at the table.

While swallowing a lump of nothing in my throat, I peer down at him.

"Don't you ever forget how much I love you, Leo!"

He glances up and smiles. "When are you going to finish the story?"

My eyes sting as I wrap my arms tightly around him. "Please don't forget me." Every ounce of me wants to stay here to watch him grow up. As I silently say goodbye to him, a ball of emotion spearheads its way to the back of my throat. My stomach clenches. I know immediately that my world has changed. I suddenly wonder if I will ever see him or Maggie again. I can't shake this feeling that I won't ever be back. Slowly, I release him from my arms, then abruptly turn towards the door. With my heart in my throat, I collect the bag from off the floor, give one last look at Leo, then walk out the door.

As I wait on the step for the stranger to arrive, I stare at the black car parked out the front of the house. A small crowd has already gathered around the shiny vehicle. Men are bent over, peering in through the windows.

The stranger walks out of the house and closes the door behind him.

"I'm sorry you had to go through that, Evie," he says, stopping on the top step next to me. "I know you'll miss them."

"Some. Yes. But not all of them." I move down the front steps.

"Here, let me take that bag for you."

"No, I can look after myself." I stride forward. The crowd parts, creating a narrow path for me to walk to the car. I climb into the back seat, safeguarding my bag on my lap. All my things are packed up as if they were nothing.

A second later, the driver gets in. The vehicle jerks forward. I hold tightly onto my bag as I'm transported away and into the unknown.

CPSIA information can be obtained
at www.ICGtesting.com
Printed in the USA
BVHW040830090223
658200BV00002B/52